THE

SALVATION OF

TRACE LOGAN

A Western

R. Annan

One Vision Publishing

The Salvation of Trace Logan
Copyright 2016 © R. Annan
WGA Reg. #R31962 (08/08/16)

Content Editor: Karren Doll Tolliver
Author's Portrait by Hazel Tertsakian
Photography © L. Annan

One Vision Publishing
Copyright 2017
ISBN: 978-1-942338-55-0 (Print)
ISBN: 978-1-942338-56-7 (eBook)

This book is a work of fiction. Any references to real events, businesses and locales are intended only to give the fiction a sense of reality and authenticity. Any resemblance to actual persons, living or dead, is entirely coincidental.

Dedicated to

Judy and Butch Trainor

Chapter 1

Getting into the bank that afternoon was easy and no one caused any trouble. In fact, everyone seemed very friendly. They said the manager was out to lunch. The customers sat quietly in a corner as the old white-haired teller stuffed thirty-five thousand dollars into Trace Logan's saddlebag with a smile on her sweet little face.

"Thank you, ma'am," Logan said.

His bandana was up over the bridge of his nose and his hat was pulled low. All she could see were the two slits of his eyes staring at her.

"Somethin' smells fishy, boss," Tuck Bannister whispered to Logan. "I think we're in a trick here."

Even Sandy Quinn, who was usually a steady hand, seemed nervous. He fastened his eyes on the open doorway as if expecting a surprise. "I got a feelin' about this, boss," he muttered.

It was a simple job on a small town cattlemen's bank in Hays City. They'd done this many times before, from Baker City, Montana, to Gloversville, Nebraska. They'd even hit a few mining towns in Colorado.

Only this time it seemed a little too easy.

"Let's go," Logan said when the teller was finished. Bannister and Quinn headed for the door with Logan coming fast behind them.

That's when the firing started.

Engels, Selby and Utley, who were outside with the horses, got hit first. Bullets started coming down from rooftops across the street and every other direction. Engels fell first, taking a bullet between the eyes. Selby got shot as he leaped into the saddle, grunting as a dozen slugs drilled into his body, slamming him to the ground. Utley got lucky and made it into the saddle without getting hit.

"Ride!" Logan yelled as loudly as he could.

Ducking low, the outlaw chief got to his mount, tossed the saddlebag over its neck and slapped it on the rump. He ran down the road alongside it, using it as a shield. Finally, he grabbed the apple and vaulted up into the saddle as bullets cut the wind all around him. He bent low over the horse's neck and held on tightly. A bullet zipped past the collar of his shirt close to his neck. He felt the heat.

"Go, Pal!" Logan yelled to his horse.

Logan's big mustang shot down the road, heading west out of Hays City. He could hear horses behind him and wondered if they belonged to the posse. A quick glance back told him it was Bannister, Quinn and Utley.

Logan's horse was a good outlaw horse. Once it got its wind and found its stride, it could run at a steady gait for hours. But he held it in reserve in case the posse got too close.

Quinn soon pulled up alongside the outlaw chief. "Utley is hit, boss!" he yelled.

Logan nodded and slowed down until Utley rode up between him and Quinn. They pulled in close to take a look. Utley was hit twice in the back.

"I'm lung-shot, boss," the young outlaw groaned.

Bannister, riding ten feet behind them, pulled his Winchester from its sheath. Holding his reins in his left hand, he twisted in the saddle and levered off three shots at the posse. They fell back a little out of range, but kept coming.

"Keep riding. It'll be dark soon," Logan cried out.

He and Quinn reached out to keep Utley from falling from the saddle. The trail cut across a field of wild rye and switch grass. Far ahead was a big stand of pines.

"We'll lose them in the trees," Logan bellowed.

Bannister kept up a steady fire until his rifle was empty and then shoved it back into its sheath. He kicked his horse in an effort to catch up with the others.

The sun was just below the top of the trees when they rode into the stand of tall pines. Once there, they slowed the horses down to a walk. Logan took the lead and Bannister came up to help with Utley. It got dark fast and the damp coolness of evening quickly set in. They found a shallow stream and stopped to rest the horses and let them drink.

Quickly dismounting, they helped Utley down off his horse. He couldn't stand or sit, so they laid him on the grass by the water's edge.

"I'm done fer," Utley said, his voice barely a whisper. He had the face of a young boy, seventeen or eighteen. He stared up at Logan. "I need ya ta do me a favor, boss."

"Sure, kid," Logan replied. He knelt by Utley and lowered his head to hear.

"My sister lives near a place called Slocum's Ridge, by the lower fork of the Smoky Hill River. Her an' her husband got a small spread there. Their name is Harnett."

"Try not to talk, kid," Logan said.

"Tell her I'm sorry an' I love her. Will ya do thet, boss? Promise?"

"Sure, kid, I'll do that for you," Logan said softly. The look on his face revealed his sorrow.

He looked up quickly. The sound of horses cut the air. It was the posse, not far away.

"Y'all best get goin'," Utley said haltingly, painfully. He coughed and blood bubbled from the corner of his mouth.

Someone suddenly shouted nearby. They had been seen. Rifles barked. Quinn grunted and fell over on his face. The bullets came fast and thick, shattering the trunks and the branches. Logan looked at Quinn. He was dead with a bullet in the back of his head. Suddenly, Utley's horse screamed and fell. Bannister jumped up and ran towards a berm for cover, but never made it. He was hit three times in the back and went stumbling into the stream.

Logan lay low and crawled to where Utley's horse lay on its side. He grabbed the rifle from its sheath and, sighting across the saddle of the dead horse, he levered six rounds back in the direction of the posse. He heard a grunt and a scream. Someone shouted to fall back.

Logan fired off the rest of the rounds and waited. Voices whispered off to his left. They were trying to take him from the side. He crouched low and crawled over to where his horse had wandered. Grabbing the reins, he led it slowly down a bank to a shallow gulch and into darker shadows, away from the posse. Once there, he waited for night to fall.

It seemed like it never would, but it finally got pitch black in the woods. Logan took the reins again. He walked quietly away, leading the mustang along. His heart pounded hard against his ribs. He kept moving.

Finally, he came out of the pines into a vast, open field of high broom sedge. Stopping there to look around, he ran his hands over his horse's body to see if it had been hit. It hadn't. He let out a sigh of relief and swung slowly up into the saddle.

"Let's go, boy," Logan whispered, bending low over the saddle. The animal walked slowly forward. Logan could barely make out the differences in the grades of darkness. He struggled to figure out what was beyond the field.

Halfway across, he remembered the saddlebag with the thirty-five thousand dollars. It was still draped across his mustang's neck. A sudden wave of guilt swept over the outlaw. All his men were dead and he was left with the money.

Logan felt their blood was on it and it wasn't worth any one of their lives.

Chapter 2

Bank robber Trace Logan rode across the lower branch of the Smoky Hill River about forty miles southwest of Hays City. His intentions were to stop at Scott City overnight, then go on to Slocum's Ridge to see Len Utley's sister and deliver his message to her. Once that was done, he figured he'd ride west into Colorado and find a quiet place there to settle down. Maybe he could get a job as deputy in some small town. Who better to enforce the laws than a lawbreaker?

The death of Utley, Engels, Selby, Quinn and Bannister made him realize the useless, dangerous life he was leading. He didn't know how or why he was alive, but thanked God for it. He should be lying dead with the others. Logan had always known that robbing banks as a full-time occupation was a dead-end trail that would eventually end with him being shot or hanged. Sometimes he had bad dreams about it. Only the very, very lucky got away without dancing at the end of a rope.

He had to stop, put it behind him and start clean, if he could.

Logan and his men had been called the Gang of Six for some reason. Sometime, somewhere, some lawman had put out a flyer to that effect. It gave a description of all of them, but there were no pictures. The name stuck, however, and the fliers and posters multiplied. And now, no one but Trace Logan knew that the Gang of Six was out of business. All but one of them had been shot to ribbons in a small cattle town in the Kansas outback, over two hundred miles west of Abilene.

As Logan rode across the lower branch of the Smoky Hill River, he thought about his future. The name, Slocum's Ridge, and the name of Utley's sister kept popping up in his mind. Maybe it was the quiet little place he was looking for, a place to start all over again with a clean slate. He had no idea where it was, but he figured he'd get directions at Scott City.

About an hour after crossing the lower branch of the Smoky, Logan rode slowly across a large field of wild rye into a stand of silver aspen. Approaching the trees, he saw three figures in an open area a few yards away.

A tall, gangly man was holding a gun on a young cowboy. Another one, short and chubby, was trying hard to get the cowboy's quarter horse under control. It appeared the kid's mount didn't like the stranger's smell and was bucking and kicking like crazy. Man and animal danced around in circles.

Both men were so busy with the kid and the horse they never noticed Logan. He dismounted forty feet away and walked slowly towards them.

"Need some help?" Logan asked the cowboy.

"I'm bein' bushwhacked!" the kid cried out. "Kin ya help me, mister?"

The man who was holding his gun on the cowboy glanced quickly at Logan with narrowed eyes. "Ride on, mister, unless yer lookin' ta eat lead!" he growled fiercely.

His partner, while keeping a tight grip on the reins of the kid's horse, fastened his eyes on Logan. "Looks like we'll soon be havin' two extra horses, pard," he grunted. "Seein' as you got the drop on thet fool, go ahead an' pop him in the belly, Gabe!"

"I reckon I'll jest do thet, Bill," Gabe chuckled.

As Gabe, the tall one, turned his gun on Logan, the outlaw's two hands moved so fast they became a blur. He fanned off a shot at the same time Gabe did. Gabe's bullet missed Logan's left ear by an inch as Logan shifted to the right and put a bullet in Gabe's chest. For a moment Gabe wondered what had happened.

"Jesus! I had him beat!" Gabe muttered, staring down at the hole in his chest.

A look of surprise came over his face and Gabe's eyes rolled up in his head. His knees buckled, his legs folded and he dropped face first in a heap on the ground.

"Ya shot my pard, ya rotten polecat!" Bill yelled as he let go of the horse's reins and went for his gun.

The young cowboy stepped back, dipped and came up with his Colt. He fanned off a single shot that knocked Bill flat on his back. After that, Bill never moved.

Logan and the kid reloaded and looked down at the bodies.

"Nice shot, kid," Logan said.

"Thanks, mister," the young cowboy replied.

"What happened?" Logan asked.

"I was asleep in the saddle when I wandered onto their camp."

Logan studied the young man's face. "I've done some sleeping in the saddle myself," he admitted. He noticed the kid's hands were shaking a little. "What's your name, kid?"

"I'm Jake Potter. What's yer handle, mister?" the cowboy asked. There was a look of panic on his face.

For a moment Logan hesitated. "Trace," he finally said, "Trace Logan." He figured no one would be able to connect him with the Gang of Six since there were no pictures on the fliers. "This yer first kill, kid?"

"Yeah," the kid said. Suddenly, he spun around, ran off behind some bushes and threw up. He came back looking drained and slightly pale, wiping his mouth. "Sorry."

"No need to apologize, kid. I did the same thing once."

"Whatta we gonna do with 'em?" Potter asked, staring down at the bodies.

Logan pondered the question as he took the makings from his shirt pocket and began to build a cigarette.

"Well, these two look pretty scrawny and rough. I don't imagine they're above the law," Logan said. "Chances are they're wanted. Might even be a small reward out on 'em."

"Scott City is about five miles west," young Potter said. "Let's take 'em an' dump 'em off at the marshal's office there."

"Sounds good. I was headed in that direction anyway, kid."

After Logan finished his smoke, they tied the two dead men over the saddles of their horses. Logan checked the saddlebags and found some old jewelry, rings, earrings, necklaces and bracelets.

"Jesus! What the heck were they? Some of this stuff still has blood on it," Logan said, frowning.

"They were cold-blooded killers, an' that's fer sure," the kid said.

11

Logan left the jewelry in the saddlebag where he found it.

They mounted up and rode out of the trees, heading west for Scott City with the bodies in tow. They passed the time making small talk as they rode along, but not asking each other any personal questions. In an hour, they crossed the railroad tracks and rode past the stables and on into town. Twenty yards up from the stables, they stopped and tied up at the marshal's office. Potter stood outside by the bodies as Logan went inside to get the marshal. A small crowd gathered around to look.

The marshal, an old man in his sixties, small and thin with silver hair and a beard, ambled out to take a look at the bodies, then went back in. Potter followed with the saddlebag and gave it to the marshal. He looked through the jewelry and nodded.

"Yep, it's them, alright, Gabe Renfrew and Bill Martin. Both are wanted fer murder and takin' women. They're worth five hundred each."

"What about the horses and gear?" Logan asked.

"I reckon it's yers ta do as ya see fit, mister."

Logan looked at the wanted posters on the wall. He spotted one about the Gang of Six.

"That wanted flier you got on the Gang of Six? You can pull it down, Marshal. They got shot up in Hays City a few days ago. I was there and saw it go down."

"Well, that's sure good news, mister," the marshal said.

Later he took them up the street to the bank to sign for the reward that had been put up by the city's businessmen and prominent citizens. It was a funny feeling for Logan to be praised by a bank manager. He and Potter split the money.

It seemed that Renfrew and Martin were two very slippery characters and had gotten away with a six-month crime spree in the area. They weren't all that smart, but they were lucky. That is, until they met Trace Logan and Jake Potter.

As for their horses and gear, Logan and the kid decided to leave it for the marshal to keep or sell as he saw fit. That made the old man act very friendly.

"Thank ya, boys," the marshal said. "It's real Christian of ya. They don't pay me all that much, ya know."

"How far is Slocum's Ridge?" Logan asked.

"Due west about thirty miles," the marshal said as Logan and Potter mounted up. "It's halfway between here and Barton Springs, on the ol' coach road. There's a sign there."

As they rode across town, Logan noticed a beanery next to a small, rundown hotel. They reined up, tied down and went in. Both ordered steaks smothered in onions with pan fried potatoes and pole beans. Apple pie and coffee followed. After that Logan leaned back in his chair and rolled a cigarette.

"Smoke?" he asked the kid.

"No thanks. Never use it."

Logan nodded and smiled. "Where ya headed, kid?"

"No place special. I'm on the drift."

"I'm goin' ta Slocum's Ridge. Do you wanna come?"

"Slocum's Ridge? Where's thet at?"

"The marshal says its west of here, on the coach road."

Potter gave it a moment's thought and nodded. "Sure, why not?" he replied. "Maybe I'll find three hots an' a cot there."

Logan nodded and said, "Maybe we both will."

The outlaw decided that for now he'd keep up the front of being a gambler on the drift. He wasn't dressed like a cowboy, so he wouldn't fool anyone by saying he was. He wanted to see where that took him. With thirty-five thousand dollars in the secret pocket of his saddle bag, he was in no rush to go anywhere. Maybe there was a small ranch someplace where he could hide out for a spell.

"I guess were both on the drift, ain't we, Logan?" Potter said. Logan noticed he looked a little sad and lost.

"I guess so," Logan replied. After a moment of silence, he said, "Let's be pards, kid."

He said this thinking of young Len Utley and how he'd died. Utley's death had signaled the end of one way of life. Meeting Potter and killing the two outlaws had signaled the start of a new one.

Potter looked at Logan in surprise. He hadn't expected Logan's offer. It took him a moment to recover. "Okay, Logan, sure. Heck, why not?"

They shook hands to seal the bargain.

Maybe there was hope and salvation somewhere down the trail for Trace Logan after all.

Chapter 3

Slocum's Ridge was once a thriving cattle town. Years ago, when a big freeze decimated the cattle business in the northwest, it almost became a ghost town. Had it not been for rancher Gabriel Spears, the town would have shriveled up and died.

Spears had a small spread and, when the freeze came, he pulled in his best breeding stock and kept them in a small sheltered valley on his Circle S spread. Bringing up hay and grain from Hays City, he was able to save enough animals to start seeding a new herd.

Many of the other ranchers weren't that savvy. Especially the new ones from the East who didn't know their backsides from their elbows when it came to raising cattle. One after another they met with disaster and foreclosure by the banks.

Spears convinced a big commercial loan bank in Kansas City that he had a small herd of prime stock and would soon be viable as a rancher again. He was so convincing that the bank allowed him a fifty-thousand dollar line of credit through the bank's branch at Scott City.

Immediately, he transferred the funds to the bank in Slocum's Ridge and bought up all the foreclosed properties. Many of them still had a dozen or so prime steers and heifers drifting aimlessly about. He mixed them with his stock and they became the seedbed for the cattle empire Spears had dreamed about.

Once he had purchased the four small ranches bordering his own spread, Spears ordered a railroad car full of barbed wire. He then had his ramrod, Dan Clegg, hire twenty of the toughest out of work cowboys he could find. That was easy since there were hundreds hanging around the cattle shipping depots all over the West.

In a few months, Spears had his vast ranch closed in by a barbed wire fence, including the three streams that ran into the lower branch of the Smoky Hill River. Every mile or so, he had a large swing gate installed in case he had to move his stock for one reason or another. His men kept an eye on the gates for rustlers.

Spears' secret mission was to ruin the other three ranchers that were still holding out, Mike Purcell, Jed Newton and Tom Harnett. Of the three, Tom Harnett, owner of the Diamond H, was the most troublesome. He was outright belligerent and rude. He openly boasted that someday he was going to kick Spears' butt from one end of the town to the other. But Harnett only said this when he was drunk and having a good time at the Silver Sparrow Saloon in Slocum's Ridge, which he visited often.

Tom Harnett had a drinking and gambling problem. Several days a week Harnett's wife Brittney and his daughter Sidney waited anxiously for him to come home. Harnett usually returned in the wee hours of the morning, smelling like whiskey and painted ladies.

Gabe Spears had met Brittney Harnett in town many times. It was mostly at church, but often at Saul Gain's Mercantile. Whenever he did, he made sure he was charming and polite to her. His ramrod, Dan Clegg, was especially polite to Harnett's young daughter. All he got for his efforts, however, was a cold stare.

As far as the law was concerned, the only law in Slocum's Ridge was old Marshal Tank Stillwell, an old ex-cowboy with a bad back and bowed legs.

At one time, Stillwell had wrangled for Spears. When he got too old and slow, Spears gave him a job as chuck wagon cook. That didn't work out too well, however, as the old man's cooking soon gave the Circle S cowboys the runs. Spears was at a loss as what to do with the old man. Then, after giving the matter much thought, Spears had an idea. One day, he cut Stillwell loose and saw that he got elected town marshal of Slocum's Ridge at thirty dollars a month. In that position he couldn't do any harm and Spears could use him whenever he wanted. As far as he was concerned he owned old Stillwell and always would.

Tank Stillwell took his new job seriously, however, and felt good about wearing a marshal's badge. He wore it proudly, but to many of the Circle S cowboys he was just a joke.

As for the real law in Slocum's Ridge, Spears' ramrod, Dan Clegg, and his cowpokes ran the town the way they saw fit and no one bucked them. That went for Stillwell, too. He dared not go against Spears or he would end up out of a job and no one would hire an old man like him.

Chapter 4

Outlaw Trace Logan and young cowboy Jake Potter rode into Slocum's Ridge on a Sunday evening. They noticed that the important places in town were open, including Aunt Martha's Beanery and Boarding House, the jail and the Silver Sparrow Saloon. There was also the Bluestem Hotel at the other edge of town. It was owned by the same man who owned the Silver Sparrow, which was businessman Fred Savage.

"Let's tie on the feedbag, kid," Logan suggested.

"Good idea. I'm as hungry as a bear."

They took their horses down to the stable by the jailhouse. A young boy came walking out of a shack to meet them.

"Give 'em both a drink, a feed and a rubdown," Logan said. He dug a quarter eagle from his pants and tossed it to the boy. He grabbed it, jammed it into his pocket and nodded.

Logan and Potter left the stables and walked up the street. They walked past the Bluestem Hotel and the Silver Sparrow Saloon. Wending their way through a Sunday evening crowd, they finally walked up on the porch of Aunt Martha's Beanery and

Boarding House. Trace looked in through a window. It was fairly packed, but he did spot an empty table near the window. He waved to the kid and they went in and sat down.

A few minutes passed and a small, buxom, pixie-like lady with blond hair, about fifty-years old, came over to their table to greet them.

"Well, bless my soul. You're the two best lookin' cowboys I ever set eyes on, so help me Sam," she said, smiling. "Howdy, strangers! I'm Aunt Martha! If yer lookin' fer a clean room for the night, yer in the right place. The rooms down at the Bluestem Hotel are full of all sorts of vermin that'll eat yer hide off. No sir, you sure don't wanna go down there."

Aunt Martha chuckled at her own banter. She had a wide grin on her cute round face. "If it's feminine companionship you two are lookin' fer," she continued, "why they're all down at the Silver Sparrow this time of day."

Logan laughed. "That's good to know, ma'am. I'll keep that in mind." There was an instant liking between them. "But what I'm looking for is the Harnett spread. Any idea where it is?"

"Well, I sure do, handsome. Follow the road west about ten miles. You'll see a big, red barn off to the left, down in a shallow spot. But you'll see the windmill long before you git there."

"Thanks, ma'am," Logan said. "I guess we'll be able to find it easy enough."

Logan and Potter ordered the house special, a bowl of beef stew with sourdough biscuits and salted lard butter. They took their time eating and sat relaxed for a while before leaving. As they stood up to leave, Martha came over to see them again.

"Y'all come back," Aunt Martha said. "And remember what I said about them rooms down at the Bluestem."

"Yes, ma'am, I sure will," Logan replied, giving her a big smile.

They saluted the little woman and went outside to stand in the brisk evening air. Violin music and voices rolled up from the Silver Sparrow. People were laughing and shouting and having a good time. The street was full of people taking an evening stroll, chatting as they walked about.

"How about we go down there and get a drink," Logan said.

"I don't drink, as a rule," the young cowboy replied.

Logan chuckled. "You don't smoke or drink. Do you swear?"

"Sometimes, when I git real mad."

"Maybe they'll have a soda pop or a weak beer."

"Well, okay, I guess a beer won't hurt."

They walked slowly down the street past drunken cowboys and sober townsfolk. Darkness was closing in and bats and night birds flew low to the ground. The glow of oil lamps came from the houses and businesses and lit up the street.

From the number of horses tied up at the rail, Logan knew the place was stuffed to the gills. He stopped to study the brands on the animals' rumps. One brand, the Circle S, outnumbered the other brands by far. He noticed one mount with a Diamond H brand. It was a dun quarter horse with a blazed forehead.

They went in through the batwing doors into a cloud of cigarette smoke and the smell of cheap whiskey. Oil lamps hung from the rafters, casting dancing shadows. The lamps above the tables showed they were filled with either poker players or cowboys with girls sitting on their laps. Bottles and glasses were piled high in the middle of them.

The kid followed Logan over to the bar where there were crocks and jars full of pickled cucumbers, hardboiled eggs in brine, beef jerky and hardtack. Logan knew everything was heavily salted to make the cowboys thirsty.

In one far corner of the Silver Sparrow there was a small, empty space large enough to accommodate a dozen dancers. An old man played an out-of-tune, three-string violin. An upside-down hat lay on the floor, close to his feet, a receptacle for donations.

Logan and Potter were just able to squeeze up to the bar and order flip-tops. The beer was made from prickly pear cactus juice. It was seasoned with lime and sugar and had a pleasant taste.

They were there no more than five minutes when a cowboy walked up to them. He was a tall, lean man with a square, hard-lined jaw. He wore a thick, black mustache over his upper lip that overlapped the sides of his mouth. His eyebrows were bushy and black, too, and hung above two blazing eyes sunk under a bulging forehead. He had a fixed sneer on his face that immediately irritated Logan.

"Who ya ridin' for?" he asked Logan. His voice was sharp and unfriendly.

"Nobody. Just passing through," Logan replied.

The cowboy stared hard at him as if trying to get inside his head and read his mind. Those piercing black eyes danced in the flickering lamp light.

"Alright," the man said coldly, "finish yer drinks and move on."

Potter sniffed and said, "We just got here, mister."

"An' yer just leavin', kid. This is a Circle S hangout."

"Who's the Circle S?" Potter asked.

"Since yer just passin' through ya don't need to know, do ya, little boy?"

"Don't call me 'little boy', mister," Potter said sharply.

There was a sudden tension between the man and Potter. Logan smiled to break the ice, saying, "Okay, friend. We get yer message. We'll finish up and leave, right, kid?"

Young Potter nodded grudgingly. "Sure. We don't want no trouble."

Just then, there was a loud bang that startled everybody. The batwing doors flew open as if someone had hit them with a sledge hammer. It sounded like a cyclone had entered the place. A figure wearing boots, pants, shirt and a vest came storming in.

It stopped a moment to adjust its gunbelt and look around as the doors kept flapping behind it. For a moment, in the pale light, Logan thought it was a short man or boy. On second glance, he saw it was a woman.

The man quickly lost interest in Logan and Potter. He turned to the woman and gave her a salute on the brim of his hat.

"Mrs. Harnett," he said, trying to block her way, "what brings you here, ma'am?"

"You know darn well why I'm here, Dan Clegg!" She looked past him, her eyes scanning the room as if searching for someone. "Where is he?"

"Where's who, ma'am?" Clegg asked lightly.

"You know darn well who I mean, Clegg!"

The man called Clegg smirked and put his elbows on the bar. "If yer lookin' fer yer husband, I think thet's him dancin' real close with his sweetheart, Clovis McBride, ma'am."

Clegg nodded at the people on the dance floor and then let out with a sadistic chuckle.

Mrs. Harnett brushed past Clegg and walked swiftly to the dance area. When the fiddle player saw her coming, he stopped playing, grabbed his hat and ducked out of sight. Logan had gotten a glimpse of Mrs. Harnett's face as she passed by. It was a beautiful face flushed with both anger and pain. It fascinated him, but he had no time to ponder it as an argument broke out on the dance floor. Accusations were shouted. Male and female voices shouted over each other for a while and then there was a sudden, deadly quiet.

A woman on the dance floor screamed and a gunshot rang out. It echoed off the walls and ceiling of the Silver Sparrow. Seconds later, something hit the sawdust-covered floor very hard.

"Jesus!" Logan said aloud. "Who got shot?"

Dan Clegg, without looking at Logan, chuckled, "She jest put a lead pill in her husband. Dead center! She finally broke."

Logan heard some scuffling and saw that two men had the Harnett woman by the arms. They dragged her out through the batwing doors. She offered no resistance, but glanced at him as they forced her outside. In those violet eyes Logan saw a silent plea for help.

"Where are they taking her?" Logan asked.

"Down to the jail," Clegg said. "She'll be charged and hung." He seemed pleased. There was that built-in sneer on his face that Logan wanted to rip off. Clegg suddenly glared at Logan and the kid. "Now you two hit the trail or you'll git the same."

"Sure," Logan said with a half-smile. "Glad to have met you, Clegg." He wanted the man to know he knew his name and wouldn't forget this meeting.

Before Clegg could answer, Logan and the kid quickly left.

Chapter 5

They stepped down off the porch of the Silver Sparrow and stood there looking back inside. The kid's face was red with anger. "Who the heck is he ta tell us what ta do like thet?"

"It's okay, kid. You gotta know when to let things slide," Logan replied. He began going from horse to horse.

"Our broncs ain't here," Potter said, "we left 'em at the stable, remember?"

"I know. I'm looking for her and her husband's horses." He finally stopped looking and untied two quarter horses. "This is theirs. These two. Both have the Diamond H burn." He led the horses down the street.

"You stealin' their horses?" Potter asked, trailing behind.

"Nope. I'm taking 'em down to the stables with ours."

"Then what?"

"Then we're going to visit the jailhouse."

"Why?"

"Don't ask so many questions, kid. Yer makin' my head hurt."

They left the horses with the stable boy and walked back up to the jail. Once there, they stood outside in the shadows, listening to the voices and sounds within. It seemed the old marshal didn't want to arrest Mrs. Harnett. He argued with the two men a while, but finally gave in. He could be heard putting her in a cell. The two men came out of the jail and walked slowly up the road to the Silver Sparrow, laughing as they went.

"Spears will be happy ta hear about this," one said as they faded into the darkness.

"Yeah! Now he can have a clear shot at her spread," the other said.

Logan waited until the men were well up the road before he and Potter went into the jailhouse. The old, bowlegged marshal was talking to the prisoner who stood gripping the bars so hard her knuckles were white.

"I'm sorry, Britt," he said. "I got no choice. I don't know much about the law, ya know?"

"It's alright, Tank," Brittney Harnett said. "It's not your doin'."

They suddenly noticed the two intruders.

"What's Dan Clegg want now, huh?" the old man asked.

"I don't work for Clegg. I'm Mrs. Harnett's lawyer. I've come to bail her out." Logan said. The fact that he wore a coat, vest and pants gave him sort of a city look.

It was almost enough to convince the old marshal, but didn't quite do the job. "So you say, mister. I don't believe a word yer sayin', do you Britt? It might be a trick ta get you out an' hang ya!"

Brittney Harnett stared suspiciously at Logan and Potter. The marshal scratched his whiskers and leered at them with squinted, watery eyes.

"How much is her bail?" Logan asked.

"Hell, I don't know," the old marshal said. "How much do ya usually give?"

"Two hundred," Logan said. He took a roll of bills out of his pocket and handed two of them to the marshal. The old man stared at the money for a moment, shrugged and then started to unlock the cell door.

'Hold it, Tank!" Brittney Harnett said. "I don't know either one of these men. Maybe Clegg did send them after all!"

The marshal pulled his gun and leveled it at Logan's belly.

"Hold it, ya varmints. Raise them hands or I'll plug ya!"

Logan and Potter ignored his command.

"Mrs. Harnett," Logan said. "I believe you had a brother. His name was Len Utley."

"Leonard? Is he here?"

"No, ma'am. We were friends. He died a week ago."

Brittney Harnett looked down at her hands for a moment, then back at Logan.

"You knew my brother?" she asked haltingly, her voice almost cracking.

Logan nodded. "Yes, I did. His last words were that I should find you and tell you how much he missed and loved you, ma'am."

Brittney Harnett stood with a pained look on her face, as if she were about to cry. Finally, she asked, "How did he die?"

Logan was about to answer quickly, but stopped. His mind searched for words that wouldn't hurt. Finally, he said, "It was an accident. He was killed in a stampede on the way up from Texas."

"Oh," Brittney Harnett said softly, holding back her tears. "Alright, Tank, let me out. They're friends."

The marshal unlocked the cell.

"I'm Trace Logan, ma'am, and this is my partner, Jake Potter. We're cowboys."

"I thought ya said ya was a danged lawyer?" the old marshal yelled. He was befuddled. "Didn't ya say thet?"

"I don't think so," Logan replied as he led Brittney Harnett outside. The marshal followed. "Your horse and your husband's horse are down at the stable, ma'am."

For a moment, old Tank Stillwell watched them walk away. He looked confused as he stood in the open doorway of the jailhouse with the two hundred dollars in his hand.

"Hey, there, hold up!" the old man suddenly yelled down the road at them. "I'll need another ten dollars to bury Tom Harnett!"

Logan dug a double eagle from his pocket and tossed it to the marshal. "Make it a decent one."

On the way to the stable, Brittney Harnett said, "I don't know who you are or why you're doing this, but I thank you, Mr. Logan. However, I have to say that you and your friend are stepping into big trouble. You should ride off while you can."

"Is it that bad, ma'am?"

"You have no idea, Mr. Logan."

They picked up their horses as well as Brittney's and her husband's horse and rode west through town. About five miles outside of Slocum's Ridge, Brittney Harnett broke down crying.

"I didn't mean to shoot Tom," she sobbed, "but I just couldn't take it anymore. His cheating was bad enough, but his gambling and drinking has just about ruined us."

Logan pulled his mount closer to hers. He could see the wetness on her face in the moonlight. It was a beautiful face that should be laughing.

"All that and the trouble Spears and Clegg are giving us. I'm about ready to sell, but Sid won't let me. She said we have to hang on. I don't see how we can."

"Who's Sid?" Logan asked.

"My daughter, Sidney," Brittney said, wiping her eyes with her right hand. She looked over at Jake Potter. "You're very quiet, Mr. Potter."

"Yes, ma'am," Potter said. "I'm a cowboy."

"Some are very loud," Brittney said.

"I'm from Texas, ma'am," Potter said with pride. "We usually don't talk all thet much."

Logan chuckled. "The kid is all action and few words, ma'am."

That at least got a smile out of Brittney Harnett.

Chapter 6

After his men had taken Brittney Harnett down to the jail and reported back to him, Dan Clegg, ramrod of the Circle S, stood at the bar of the Silver Sparrow Saloon with that fixed sneer on his face, smirking with satisfaction. The Harnett woman had just signed her own death warrant. Now it would be easier for his boss, Gabe Spears, to grab the Diamond H Ranch. With her husband out of the way, she and her young daughter Sidney would never be able to run the ranch or meet the mortgage payments. Spears hated Tom Harnett and Clegg had planned to kill him all along, but now she had done the job for him.

Clegg tossed down his shot of whiskey, walked out of the Silver Sparrow Saloon and headed down the street to the Bluestem Hotel.

He went in and walked up to the desk clerk in the foyer. "Is Mr. Spears in, Bill?" he asked.

Bill nodded and Clegg hurried upstairs to room number eight, the one reserved for his boss. He stood at the door listening for a moment then tapped gently against it with his knuckles.

"It's me, boss," Clegg said in a low voice.

Clegg waited until the rancher answered before quickly opening the door and letting himself in. Spears was sitting on the edge of the bed half dressed. Behind him, Gail Simpson's beautiful head stuck out above the covers. She smiled at Clegg and he nodded back, not saying anything.

"Hi, Dan," Gail said in a soft, seductive voice. Clegg ignored her and looked over towards Spears.

"What is it, Dan?" Spears asked. He didn't seem too pleased to have Clegg barging in on him like this.

"Brittney Harnett jest shot an' killed her husband in the Silver Sparrow. She caught him dancing with Clovis McBride," Clegg replied.

Spears took a moment to absorb the news. "Where is she now?" he asked. Suddenly he was interested. Clegg was forgiven.

"I had her taken down to the jail," the ramrod boasted. "We'll hang her in the morning, after a quick trial."

"Good. Very good, Dan." Spears reached over to a chair where his shirt, vest and coat were. He got a cigar from the pocket of the vest, lit it and nodded.

Clegg started to say something about making things easier now, but Spears cut him off.

"Why don't you go back to the Sparrow," Spears said. He reached into his pants pocket and handed Clegg several double eagles. "Buy the boys a couple of rounds on me. We'll talk later."

"Sure, boss," Clegg said smiling. He took the money, glanced at the woman and left.

"What's that all about, Gabe?" Gail Simpson asked.

"Nothing to worry your pretty little head about, darling."

Spears looked down at her. She was a blonde beauty well under twenty years old. He had met her at a bar in Hays City. She was originally from a small town in Nebraska. After a wild weekend together he brought her back to Slocum's Ridge.

Gail Simpson was a breath of fresh air compared to his wife, Cindy, who, like him, was in her fifties. Cindy had never given him a child and he was disappointed over that. He had set the young girl up in a room at the Bluestem Hotel and kept her there as his mistress. It didn't take long for Cindy to find out. But, being weak-willed, she suffered the pain of it and went on as if nothing had changed.

A smallish, round-bodied man, Spears looked more like a banker or a lawyer than a rancher. Lately, he took to wearing a city suit. Most of the time he hung around the Cattlemen's Association Building, leaving the running of the ranch to his trusty ramrod, Dan Clegg. Once known as an aggressive rancher, Spears was seen now as cultivating an image of being a wealthy cattle baron. Most people feared Spears than liked him.

After Clegg left, Spears finished dressing. Gail Simpson jumped from the bed, ran to him and played her little game. She threw her arms around his neck and kissed him.

"Don't go, Gabe," she purred. "I can't stand bein' without you, honey." She had learned how to get what she wanted by playing up to him.

"I know, my love," Spears said, staring at her sweet face. She was as tall as he was. "It's hard on me, too."

"Can't we be together, darlin'? Jest you an' me, makin' love all the time?" She knew what he liked to hear.

Spears gently pried her arms away. "We will, my sweet, we will. Real soon. But I must go now, darling."

She made him talk silly like that even though it made him feel a little stupid. He enjoyed her attention.

"Until tomorrow, then," Gail said, as if her heart were breaking.

Spears kissed her and left. She listened as his boots echoed down the hall. When she couldn't hear them anymore, she broke out laughing, went to the chair and picked up the money he had left her. She put it in her purse and lay down on the bed.

Half an hour later the door opened and a young cowboy named Sam Hill of the Flying R Ranch came in. She rushed into his arms.

As for the rancher, after leaving the Bluestem Hotel, Gabe Spears rode slowly back to his ranch. He felt good about himself. Things were bending his way. Soon he would have the Harnett spread and he wouldn't even have to lift a finger to make it happen.

It was after midnight when he put his horse in the corral and went into the large, white, two-story ranch house on his Circle S spread. The place was deserted. Just about all the hands were in town with Clegg. Spears went into the den and lit an oil lamp.

"How's that whore of yours doing, Gabe, darling?"

The rasping voice gave Spears a start. He turned to see the skin and bones body of his wife, Cindy. She was sitting in a chair in a corner, dressed in a sheer nightgown, naked underneath. The women's long, straggly, gray-white hair hung down to her waist. Her intense eyes burned like hot coals in their sockets. They contrasted against her pale, shiny skin which was drawn tight across her sharp cheek bones.

Cindy Spears held a whiskey bottle in one hand. It was half empty and he could smell the alcohol on her breath, even from where she sat, ten feet away.

"You're soused," was all Spears could think of saying.

His wife struggled up on weak legs, wobbled up to him and tried to kiss him.

"Get away from me, you lush!" he said, shoving her away. She stumbled backwards, but managed to stay on her feet, grinning at him.

He blew the lamp out, walked into the dark hall and started up the stairs. She came stutter-stepping behind him on her bare feet.

"I'll never divorce you, Gabe. You're mine forever, my dear, until death us do part!" She took a swig from the whiskey bottle and let out a high-pitched laugh.

Spears stopped on top of the landing, turned and looked down at his wife. She struggled upward on unsteady legs. Halfway to the top, she stopped for a moment to gasp for air. Glaring up at him, she laughed insanely again before starting out once more, forcing herself slowly up, one step at a time. She finally reached the top and stood there weaving back and forth, completely exhausted, wheezing loudly.

"I know about her," she screamed, "but you'll never be free of me, Gabe! Never! Never! You'll be mine until you're dead! Do you hear me?"

Spears was about to walk away but stopped to stare at his wife for a moment. Suddenly he let out an angry cry and shoved her hard. Cindy Spears' frail body went flying down the stairs until it hit the floor with a sickening thud. She lay there twisted and still.

Spears stood looking down at the broken body with a look of surprise. Could it be that easy? It seemed like it. Yes. A simple shove had solved the problem. Fate had set the stage and he had taken the necessary action. This was how it was supposed to be.

Now it would be just he and Gail, together for always.

Spears stared at the body of his wife for a long time before he walked slowly down the stairs and stood over its lifeless form. He suddenly felt elated. No one else had seen what had happened. No one would ever know what he had done. This had, indeed, been his lucky night. He couldn't have wished for more. Now he could start a new life with Gail.

He decided to leave the body where it lay, undisturbed. In the morning he would send one of the men into town to bring the marshal out to the ranch.

As he walked back upstairs, a thought struck him that made him giggle. He would no longer have to eat Cindy's horrible cooking. Not ever again. She was a bad cook and had no imagination. Not like the cook in that small restaurant in Hays City where Cindy and he used to eat when he took her shopping. What was his name? Oh, yes, Jeffries. He was a superb cook. After meals he would put down a hat and play an old, worn-out violin just to pick up a little extra money. Waltzes were his specialty and he got people dancing.

Spears wondered if he could entice the young man to come and prepare meals for himself and Gail. It would be wonderful if, after the evening meal, Jeffries could play waltzes for him and her to dance by. Money would be no problem. Spears would offer to double his salary, even triple it.

Later, in bed, thoughts of Cindy Spears were eventually replaced by visons of Spears dancing with Gail to the tune of a waltz being played by the cook, Jeffries.

Chapter 7

The Diamond H spread was ten miles southwest of the old Hays City coach road. The three riders were about a hundred yards from the ranch house when they saw the dull light of an oil lamp in the kitchen windows. Using that as a beacon, they rode slowly down a slope and were soon in the yard. Just as Brittney Harnett, Trace Logan and Jake Potter rode into the yard, someone came out and stood on the porch in the shadows. Light from the windows glinted off the barrel of a shotgun.

A voice came from the porch. "Who's there?" It sounded like a young girl.

"It's me, Sid," Brittney replied.

"Who's with you, Dad?"

"No. I'm with some friends. Put your gun down."

They dismounted and walked up on the porch, leaving the horses to wander down to the water trough and then into the barn to the grain bin.

Sidney Harnett gave her mother a hug. "Where's Dad?" Sidney asked.

"Let's go inside, Sid," Brittney said. "We'll talk there."

They went into the kitchen of the two-story clapboard ranch house. An oil lamp on the kitchen table threw flickering light around the room and against the walls. Sidney Harnett glanced suspiciously at the two strangers as she went about making coffee on the big cast-iron stove. Jake Potter, in turn, couldn't take his eyes off the girl's tied-back, chestnut colored hair and large, blue eyes. She was a fair-skinned beauty that took his breath away.

"So, where's Dad?" Sidney asked again. Oddly, Logan detected no concern in her voice. It was a flat, open question.

"Your father had an accident," Logan said before Brittney could answer, not knowing why he said it. The moment the words were out, he knew he had butted in on a private matter that was none of his business.

"Oh," the girl replied sullenly, "I thought maybe Momma shot him this time. She said she would."

For a moment Logan was stunned. She sounded serious.

"I did," Brittney said. "He was dancing with that woman agin." She covered her face with her hands and began to cry. A moment later she got herself under control and stopped. "I warned him about that. What was I to do? Take it like a whipped dog?" she asked, sniffing. "I had enough, Sid!"

Sidney rushed over to her mother. They embraced each other, sobbing.

"Gee, Mom," Sidney said, tears running down her face, "I guess this means Dad don't get ta beat us any more, don't it?" She laughed nervously and pulled back, wiping her face with her hands. She looked at Logan and Potter. "I'm sorry."

"No need ta be sorry, Miss Sidney," Potter said.

"I guess we'll be going now, ma'am," Logan said softly, feeling like an intruder.

Brittney turned to her daughter. "Mr. Logan got me out of jail. I owe him two hundred dollars. And a double eagle, too."

"There's no hurry about that, ma'am," Logan said.

"Would you like to stay for coffee?" Sidney asked, looking directly at Potter. She held him helpless with her blue-eyed gaze. She practically had the young cowboy hypnotized.

Potter looked over at Logan and said eagerly, "We sure would, wouldn't we, pard?" Logan saw his condition and nodded.

They sat at the table talking and were soon drinking coffee and eating crullers. Their talk was of no importance, just idle banter to get the measure of each other. The girl and Potter were a contrast. Sidney Harnett was outgoing, whereas Jake Potter was shy and reserved.

"You don't talk much, Mr. Potter," Sidney said.

"He's from Texas, Sidney," Brittney said. "He told me."

"What's he doin' way up here?" the girl asked.

Potter cleared his throat to speak. "I came up on a cattle drive from the Frio River, near Uvalde."

"There's gotta be more to the story than that," Sidney said.

Potter nodded. "One day I figured I'd had enough of wranglin' cows and decided ta go off on my own ta see things. Well, I didn't see much, but I did git into some trouble. Mr. Logan happened along jest as I was bein' bushwhacked by a couple of sidewinders."

Sidney Harnett frowned and said, "That's a pitiful story, Mr. Potter. You need someone to put a harness on you so you don't go straying off by yourself and getting into trouble."

Logan smiled and replied, "I've got him on a short rope now, ma'am."

It felt good to be sitting there in the coziness of the kitchen with these two women and talking about unimportant things. Time passed quickly.

An hour or so later, Logan stood up, stretched and yawned. Brittney Harnett stared at the tall, lean man dressed like a gambler who claimed he was a cowboy.

"Where are you headed, Mr. Logan?" she asked.

"I don't rightly know, ma'am. Maybe I'll head back to Hays City."

"That's a long way off to be starting this late. Why don't you and Mr. Potter stay overnight in the bunkhouse? It's empty."

Logan thought about that remark for a moment then asked, "I hope you don't take offense in my asking, ma'am, but why is that?"

Brittney looked away for a moment, then replied with a sigh, "My husband didn't pay the cowhands for the last three months, so they left."

"Who's tending to the cattle?"

"Well, no one. But there aren't that many left anyway."

"I see," Logan said. He looked at Potter. "How about it, kid? You as tired as I am?"

"I'm so tired I could fall asleep on a bed a-cactus," the kid replied.

Logan turned to Brittney. "We'll take you up on that offer, ma'am, and be grateful for it. Thank you."

Later, in the empty bunkhouse, the two men talked. "These two women are in a bad fix," Potter said. "I feel sorry for 'em. I surely do."

Logan stared at the young cowboy. "It's the girl, isn't it kid? She tightened your cinch, didn't she?"

Potter blushed a bit and shrugged. "I reckon maybe she did cinch me up a little bit."

"Well, I guess we could find some lame excuse to stick around a while, if you want to."

Potter smiled and his eyes lit up. "That would be great, pard! Jest great!"

"I figured it would be, kid," Logan chuckled.

Logan said no more. He lay on his bunk wondering if there was a way that he could help the Harnett women. If the truth be told, Brittney had tightened his cinch a little, too.

Chapter 8

Gail Simpson listened to the words she never hoped to hear. "How would you like to move in with me?" Gabe Spears asked. She knew it was an order, not an offer. His request came unexpectedly. Any change in her life now would upset the status quo.

The young girl had been having the best of both worlds, with a sugar daddy at one end and a lover at the other. Spears' wife had only recently died from her horrible accident. Moving out to the Circle S spread would surely complicate things. That would completely cut her off from seeing Sam Hill.

"Gee, Gabe," Gail said. "Yer wife has been dead only a week now. It wouldn't look right, would it?"

Spears thought about that, then nodded. "Alright. I suppose we could wait another week."

"Sure we kin, Gabe. I'm right here. I ain't goin' nowhere."

As he dressed, the young girl got off the bed, went over and embraced him. She looked adoringly up into his eyes, as if he were the only man in her life. The rancher stared at her and put a hand to her neck. His fingers closed around her delicate, white throat.

"Make sure you don't go anywhere, baby," he said coldly. "I'll find you no matter where you go."

Gail suddenly felt frightened. This was the first time that Spears had ever threatened her. But since his wife's death he had changed. He was brooding and dark, even sadistic. Also, he was getting rough in their love making. He had never done that before, and it scared her.

Rumors were circulating around town about the death of his wife. Some stories hinted that her fall wasn't all that accidental, that he wanted to get Cindy out of the way so he could bring his mistress out in the open. Almost everyone knew about her. A few people even knew about her lover, Sam Hill. It was a dangerous situation for her to be in. It could explode any moment.

Gail Simpson took Spears' hand from her throat and kissed its open palm, trying to calm him down. "I'll always be your girl, Gabe," she whispered softly in his ear. "You know that."

"Make sure you are, my love."

"Don't you trust me, Gabe?"

"Sure, baby, I trust you." The rancher replied sarcastically, a smirk on his face. He turned from her and finished dressing.

She felt relieved when he finally left to go back to the Circle S Ranch. Since the death of his wife he had been acting strange. This sudden change in him frightened her.

When the young cowboy Sam Hill came to her an hour later, she ran trembling into his arms. "I'm scared, Sam."

"What's the matter? Did he hurt you?"

"A little," she said. "He's gettin' mean. An' he wants me ta stay out at the ranch with him fer good."

The cowboy suddenly looked deeply concerned. "If ya do thet, baby, I won't be able ta see ya anymore!"

"What'll we do, Sam?"

Sam Hill went quiet, staring at the door as if fearing Spears would come in and find them together. He, too, was frightened.

"I'll think of something," Hill said. "We need more money. See if ya kin git more out of him."

"Alright, I'll try," she said.

It was past midnight when Spears put his horse in the corral and went into his den to have a nightcap. He kept a supply of choice bourbon from Kentucky in his lower desk drawer. After lighting the lamp on the desk, he sat down, poured a drink and lit a cigar.

Settling back comfortably in his chair, the rancher tried to evaluate just where he was at this point in his life. He was rich and successful and had a young mistress. As for the townsfolk, they respected him as a leader and valued his guidance. He was the one they came to for advice and consent.

Right after his wife's death, a feeling of impending danger had descended upon him. He couldn't put his finger on it. It was a feeling of strangeness, as if someone put a hex or curse on him. Cindy was deep into that sort of thing. She liked to read books about curses and witchcraft, signs and spells. To him it was all gibberish and nonsense. He made up his mind he would burn every bit of it.

Tonight that ominous feeling was gone and he felt great. As he drank and enjoyed his cigar, a sense of euphoria came over him. He felt very relaxed and calm, so much so that he started to nod off. Then, the next thing he knew, he felt heat and smelled something burning. He quickly realized he had dropped his cigar on the rug and now it was on fire and so was the left leg of his trousers.

Overcome with panic, Spears yelled and leaped up from his chair. He began stomping on the flames, dancing around in circles and crying out in pain. It took a while before he finally got the fire out, but even so it had left a black spot on the rug. There was also a small burn on his foot, as well as his left leg. He had never done this before and couldn't understand how it had happened so quickly.

Finally, he stood staring down at the rug. For a moment, the black spot seemed to form into the profile of Cindy's face, but when he blinked and rubbed his eyes it disappeared. It was his imagination playing tricks on him.

Satisfied that the fire was out, he blew out the lamp on his desk and walked out into the dark hallway. He stopped for a moment to look down at the place where his wife Cindy had lain after her fall down the stairs. There were several small, round, dark spots, a residue of her blood, on the carpet there. Spears shrugged and walked slowly up the stairs.

Halfway to the top, he pulled to a stop. A look of fear come over his face. He turned to stare downward with widened eyes, thinking he had heard a voice. Not any voice. No, it was as if Cindy had whispered his name. "Gabe...Gabe...Gabe!" Her voice seemed to float up from the dark hole at the bottom of the stairs. A sudden surge of cold fear sent him pounding up the steps. At the top, he heard it again. He put his hands over his ears and ran into his bedroom. Once there, he locked the door and jammed a chair against it.

He sat on the bed shaking for a long time before getting undressed. He didn't sleep very well that night.

Chapter 9

It was their fourth day at the Diamond H Ranch. After a quick look around and sizing up the place, Logan and Potter decided it was all over for Brittney Harnett and the Diamond H spread. They had come to the end of their tether.

Jake Potter turned to Trace Logan. "Mrs. Harnett is in a bad fix."

"Yeah," Logan replied, "I know, kid. She's just about hangin' on by a saddle strap." There was no way out of her predicament that Logan could think of.

"Sid said the bank won't give her mom anymore credit because her dad didn't make payments on a past loan he took out."

"How much was the loan for?"

"It was for five hundred dollars," Potter replied.

"Sid said that, did she?"

"Yep, that's what she said."

"Anything else?"

"They're plumb broke. They'll have ta sell. There's a big rancher named Gabe Spears who wants ta buy the Diamond H out."

"Who's Spears, did she say?"

"Yeah, he's a rancher who owns the big Circle S spread nearby. He's well known in town. Practically runs and owns it."

"That's bad," Logan said. "Really bad."

"How come?"

"All Spears has to do is buy up that five-hundred dollar debt and put a lien on this place. That'll make him part owner. He could demand payment. She'd have to sell the ranch to pay him off."

"Yeah," Potter said. "I guess she would, wouldn't she?"

"I'm goin' into town, kid," Logan said.

"What fer?"

"I'm gonna buy up that debt before this guy even thinks about it."

"You gonna use yer reward money?"

"Yeah."

"Take my half."

"No, I got plenty extra."

Potter laughed. "What did ya do, rob a bank?"

Logan adjusted his gunbelt and said, "I got lucky one night in a poker game up in Stockton."

The kid scratched his head. "If you buy up thet paper, then you'll own a piece of the Diamond H, won't ya?"

"Yeah, I suppose I will, won't I?"

"I'll go with ya."

"I'd like it better if you stayed here, kid. Keep an eye peeled for trouble."

"Alright."

Logan saddled up and rode for Slocum's Ridge. In little over an hour he was sitting in the bank buying up the Harnett debt. The manager, Arnold Foley, looked at him suspiciously.

"If I might ask," Foley said, "are you a friend of Mrs. Harnett, or what?"

"I knew her husband," is all Logan offered.

"Oh."

Logan thought of something and asked, "How much would you say the Diamond H spread is worth?"

"Well, it's a small ranch, about five hundred sections. Big enough for maybe 15,000 head of cattle. A low bid might come in at $32,000 at two dollars an acre," Mr. Foley said.

"Did they ever own 15,000 head of cattle?"

"Yes, they did once, a few years back, before the freeze came. It was a horrible thing to see. It just about wiped out the small ranches. Most were lucky to have ended up with a few hundred head."

"It seems like Spears did alright."

"Oh, yes. Mr. Spears is a very resourceful man. He's on his way to a full financial recovery. In three years he expects to have a herd of 25,000 head."

"In three years, huh?" Logan asked.

"Yes, at least. Maybe sooner."

"Thanks, Mr. Foley."

"It was a pleasure doing business with you, Mr. Logan."

Logan put the paperwork in his coat pocket and stood up. He and the bank manager shook hands. At that moment Gabe Spears walked into the bank.

"Hello, Mr. Spears," Foley said. He suddenly ignored Logan and concentrated on the rancher. "What can I do for you, sir?"

"Arnold, I'm here to buy up the debt on the Harnett ranch."

"Well, I'm afraid you're a bit late, sir," Foley said sheepishly. "A friend of Mr. Harnett has already taken care of that matter."

Spears looked Logan up and down for a moment. "Who are you, sir?" Spears said coldly.

"Trace Logan, a friend of Tom Harnett."

"I'll give you double what you paid, Mr. Logan," Spears said emphatically, his eyes fixed on Logan.

Logan stalled, pretending to think it over, then shook his head. "Ah, no thanks, Mr. Spears."

"I'll make it triple!" Spears blurted out, this time almost sounding as if he were begging.

Logan scratched his head, pretending he was giving the offer some deep thought. "I'll have to talk it over with Mrs. Harnett," he finally said. "See what she wants to do."

Spears did not like that answer. He was used to getting his way.

"You'll be sorry, Mister Logan!" Spears suddenly shouted without warning, his face turning purple with rage. Everyone in the bank looked in his direction, startled by his outburst. They had never seen him looking so angry before. Giving Logan an ugly glare, the rancher went stomping outside and down the street.

The bank manager stared at Logan with a puzzled look. "That was a very generous offer," he said. "Very generous indeed, Mr. Logan."

"Yeah," Logan replied, "maybe too generous, don't you think?" He shook the bank manager's hand again and left.

After a quick lunch at Martha's Beanery, Logan rode out for the Diamond H Ranch. It was mid-afternoon when he arrived. He found Potter, Brittney and her daughter in the kitchen. Brittney fixed him with a cold stare.

"Mr. Potter tells me you went to town to buy up my debt, Mr. Logan. Is that so?"

"Yes, ma'am."

"Why?"

"Do you know a man named Spears?"

"Yes. Don't change the subject. Why did you buy my debt?"

"A second after I bought up your debt, Spears came into the bank to do the same. He offered me three times what I paid for it. Why?"

Brittney said forcefully, "Because he wants the Diamond H, that's why."

Logan got the paperwork from his shirt pocket and handed it to Brittney.

"He can't touch you now. It's yours. Take it as a gift, Mrs. Harnett."

Brittney stared at the document Logan was holding out to her. "No, I can't do that." Her voice broke as she spoke.

"I'll never put a lien on your land, Mrs. Harnett. I swear to you," The outlaw said.

Brittney looked sadly at Logan with moist eyes. He could see her pride was hurt. "I'm not helpless, Mr. Logan."

"I know that, ma'am," Logan said, "but pride and stubbornness won't save your ranch. Only money can do that. Your husband left you at that man's mercy, but now he can't touch you. Here, take this."

Sidney walked over to her mother and held her hand.

"He's right, Momma! Take it." She turned to Logan. "Thank you, Mr. Logan. We'll find a way ta pay you back, I promise."

Brittney Harnett sighed. She stared at Logan.

"Who are you, sir? You saved me from jail and a hanging, and now you save my ranch. Who are you?"

Suddenly they heard horses pounding up the road and into the yard. Sidney rushed out through the hallway and onto the porch. She watched as four armed men dismounted and stood staring up at her.

One man wore a marshal's badge. All of them rode horses with the Circle S brand. The one with the badge stepped forward and pointed a finger at Sidney.

"Are you Brittney Harnett?" he demanded with authority.

Before Sidney could answer, Brittney, Logan and Potter came quickly out onto the porch.

"I'm Brittney Harnett," she answered. "What do you want with me?"

"I come ta arrest ya, Mrs. Harnett."

"You work for Spears, don't you?" Brittney said. "I think I've seen you before."

The men shifted nervously on their feet.

"They're all Spears men, Momma," Sidney said.

"Where is Marshal Stillwell?" Brittney asked.

"He got fired, ma'am," the man with the badge said. "I'm the new marshal now, an' I've come to arrest ya."

"Why? I'm out free on bail."

"Thet was illegal. Marshal Stillwell shouldn't a-done thet. Now I gotta put ya back in until the trial."

"When is the trial?"

"That ain't decided yet. So, jest you come along, now, an' there won't be no trouble."

Logan stepped down into the yard. Potter followed and stood a few feet to his right. "Ma'am," Logan said. "Please take Miss Sidney back into the house."

Brittney hesitated for a moment and then nodded. She took Sidney by the arm and they started walking into the house.

"Stop where you are, Mrs. Harnett!" the marshal yelled.

"Keep going," Logan said calmly, dropping his hand down by his gun. He put a few more feet between him and the kid.

"I'll take the two on the left," Potter said loudly, so they all could hear.

The marshal stepped forward two steps and leered at Logan. "Move aside!" His voice cracked a little. "This is law business. She's my prisoner!"

"Mister, you can ride out or die right here," Logan growled. "Take your choice, but do it quick."

The man with the badge suddenly looked scared. Logan saw his Adam's apple dance as he swallowed hard and looked around for support. He got none.

"Jesus," one of the others cried. "Let's git the hell outta here. Thet's Trace Logan. I saw him in action once, over by Danville, near the Devil's Den. You'd be crazy ta pull on him. I'm getting' the hell outta here. Neither Dan Clegg nor Gabe Spears is payin' me enough ta eat lead."

The four men backed slowly off and carefully mounted up, keeping their hands away from their guns.

"Clegg ain't gonna like this," the one with the badge yelled back as they rode away.

Potter looked at Logan with a questioning stare. "What did he say about you, Logan?" Potter asked.

"Nothing. He was mistaken, kid," Logan said as he walked up on the porch. They all went into the house.

Chapter 10

It was late afternoon on a Friday. Spears was in his den listening impatiently as his ramrod told him what had happened out at the Diamond H spread. "You mean to tell me four men couldn't arrest one woman?"

"They said she had backup, a gunslinger and a kid from Texas."

"What gunslinger?"

"A drifter named Trace Logan."

"Logan? He must be the man I met at the bank. He paid up the debt on the ranch," Spears said. He paused a moment. "Where's the marshal?"

"Stillwell? He left town, as far as I know. Disappeared."

"Good riddance to the useless old fart. From now on keep Barns on as marshal."

"Don't you need the town council's okay?"

"As long as I'm paying the salary, they don't care who's marshal."

Clegg chuckled. Suddenly a thought struck him. "Ah, about yer girl," Clegg said, "well, I been keepin' an eye on her like you told me to."

"And?"

"Well, it turns out she's playing around with a young cowboy from one of the ranches. His name is Sam Hill."

"What? Are you sure about that, Clegg?" Spears asked. His face took on an intense look.

"Yeah, boss. One of the men told me, so I checked it out. Seems like he goes in after you leave."

Spears looked away for a moment. He had just been branded a cuckold by one of his own men. He wondered how many in town knew about Gail's young cowboy lover. "How soon after I leave?" he asked.

"Half hour. Sometimes longer," Clegg replied.

Spears got up and walked over to the window. He stood with his back to Clegg, pretending to stare out into the yard. His face was a mask of tortured anguish. He clenched his fists and gritted his teeth.

"Whatta ya want me ta do about him, boss?" Clegg asked.

Spears got his emotions under control and turned around to face Clegg. "Brace him," he replied calmly.

"Alright. What about her? Ya want her gone, too?"

"No, bring her here, bag and baggage. Sign her out of the hotel. She'll be living here now."

"Alright."

"Can you find him, this Sam Hill?"

"Sure, he usually comes into the Silver Sparrow Friday evenings. He'll drink there, waiting for you to leave town, then head over to her place."

"Alright, brace him after I leave her tonight, then go and get her."

Clegg nodded. "Consider it done, boss."

An hour later Clegg and two of his men rode into Slocum's Ridge with Gabriel Spears. They stopped at the Silver Sparrow Saloon while Spears went on to the Bluestem Hotel to see Gail Simpson.

Sam Hill stood waiting in an alleyway across from the hotel. When he saw Spears go in to visit Gail, he walked slowly up to the Silver Sparrow Saloon. Once inside, he stood at the bar nursing a drink while he watched the clock behind the bar. The young cowboy knew Spears usually stayed at the hotel about an hour and then headed for home. Once Spears had left and the coast was clear, he'd go see Gail.

Hill was sipping his drink when Dan Clegg came walking up alone from the back of the saloon. The Circle S ramrod stood directly behind him, staring at the back of the young cowboy's neck. Finally, Hill saw Clegg's reflection in the mirror behind the bar and turned slowly around.

"Hi, Clegg, long time no see," the young cowboy said, smiling nervously. He sensed something was wrong.

Clegg didn't smile back. "I hear you been callin' me names behind my back, Hill."

The young cowboy was startled and shaken. He knew Clegg and his reputation. He also knew he had been found out and that Spears had sent Dan Clegg to brace him.

"She loves me, Dan," Hill said.

"You knew she was taken, kid," Clegg said. "Ya shoulda kept yer hands off her."

The young cowboy nodded. It was plain to see that he was scared. A crowd had gathered to see the killing.

"God knows I tried, Dan." Hill said. "I just couldn't stay away. I love her, Dan."

"You knew Spears wouldn't let it stand, kid."

"Yeah, guess I did." Hill looked away for a moment, then back. He smiled weakly. "One more drink, Dan?"

"Sure, kid," Clegg said. "It's on me."

"Thanks."

The young cowboy ordered another shot of rotgut. The barman poured it slowly. He looked into Hill's eyes, seeing the look of resignation there. Hill already knew he was a dead man. He picked up his drink, turned and held his glass up high to the waiting, watching crowd.

"To Gail Simpson," the cowboy said loudly. "I'll love her 'till the day I die, an' I'll still love her when I come crawlin' through the gates of hell!"

He had just told the town that Spears was having him killed over Gail Simpson. By tomorrow it would be all over Slocum's Ridge and beyond.

"Why, you tricky skunk!" Clegg growled. He drew and shot the young cowboy in the heart. The shot glass dropped out of Sam Hill's hand, hit the floor and shattered.

Everyone who saw it knew it was murder, plain and simple. Those that didn't see it would know by sundown the next day. This was one secret Spears couldn't hide.

Chapter 11

On Saturday morning everyone was in the kitchen having breakfast. Brittney Harnett turned to her daughter Sidney, "I have to go into town."

"What for, Momma?" Sidney asked.

"Sugar, salt and flour. Also, some baking powder."

Logan looked up from his coffee cup. "That's not such a good idea, ma'am. Spears will have men waiting to ambush you."

"I'll go, then," Sidney offered. "They're not after me."

Logan thought about that for a moment. "They might grab you, just to get at your mother."

Young Potter spoke up. "I'll go with her, if thet's okay."

Sidney shrugged. "If you want to, fine. It's not like I can't take care of myself, you know."

"I need some shells, anyway," Potter said.

"Oh, okay," Sidney replied "in that case you can come along."

The two young ones tried to act as if they didn't care about each other, but it was easy to see they did. Even a stranger could see through their game of youthful indifference.

Brittney looked at Logan. "Maybe you should go with them. Just in case there's trouble."

"That would leave you here alone. Spears might have some spies out, waiting just for that."

"You think so?"

"I wouldn't risk it, ma'am."

"Alright, then." Brittney paused a moment, then turned to her daughter. "Tell Mr. Gains to put it on our account," she said.

Later, as Potter hitched up the buckboard, Logan took him aside and handed him fifty dollars. "Don't let her pay for it, kid."

"I wasn't goin' to."

"And pay off their account."

"Alright."

Potter took the reins and they rode out of the Diamond H yard onto the road to Slocum's Ridge. It was a fine day and the sun was finding its way across a blue sky piled high with big, cotton clouds. Sidney sat stiffly and looked ahead, acting as if Potter were a chauffeur and she was the lady. They hardly spoke to each other.

They rode into town just after noontime. Two of Dan Clegg's men stood smoking on the porch of the Silver Sparrow watching them pass by. The tall, slim one was Randy Fuller and the shorter, stockier one was Tom Underwood.

"That's her," Fuller said. "The gunslinger ain't with her, but the kid is."

"Yeah, I see her," Underwood replied. "I sure do. Pretty little Sidney Harnett and thet green kid. How about thet?"

Fuller chuckled. "I'd like ta see jest how green the kid is, Tom. I really would."

"So would I, pard," Underwood replied with a chuckle.

"Why don't we go down there and shake his tree, Tom?"

"Heck yeah, let's do it," Underwood said.

Fuller, who already had a few drinks under his belt, sniffed. He wiped his nose on the back of his hand, adjusted his gunbelt and stepped down into the street. Fastening his eyes on the Harnett buckboard, he headed straightaway in its direction.

"You comin'?" Fuller called back without turning around.

Underwood shrugged and sighed. He had no choice. If Fuller told Clegg he didn't back him up, there would be hell to pay.

"Yeah, I'm a-comin'," Underwood replied as he hurried up alongside Fuller. Fuller pulled his gun and checked the load.

"You full?" Fuller asked.

Underwood patted his holster. "Yeah, I'm full."

They walked slower now, watching as Potter pulled the buckboard up in front of the loading platform at Gain's Mercantile. He helped Sidney down and stood watching as she mounted the steps. She stopped on the platform and turned to look at him.

"Come in with me."

"Alright, sure."

The went into the store together. Saul Gains came from the back and greeted them. "How is your mother doing, Sidney?" Gains was a small, frail man with a wide smile on his cherry-red face.

"Fine, Mr. Gains," Sidney said as she handed him the list of things her mother needed. He quickly went about measuring out the correct amounts. Finally, he added up the charge.

"Can you put it on our account, Mr. Gains?"

"Of course," Gains replied and took out a large ledger. He wrote some figures in it.

"We can go now, Mr. Potter," Sidney said to the cowboy.

"You go ahead, Miss Sidney," the cowboy answered. "I have to buy a box of shells. I'll bring the groceries."

"Alright," Sidney replied. She said goodbye to Mr. Gains and left the store.

Potter waited until she was outside. "How much is their account?"

"Twenty-five dollars."

Potter handed Gains the fifty dollars Logan had given him. "Spread this out on their account."

Gains looked curiously at the young cowboy for a moment, then nodded and smiled. He took this generous gesture to mean the cowboy was interested in Sidney.

"I see," he said suggestively. "Good luck, young man."

Potter blushed a little and picked up the bags of groceries.

As he walked away, he heard voices outside by the buckboard. It sounded as if Sidney was talking to some people. He stopped for a moment, undecided as to what to do. He wondered if it was some of Spears' men. Perhaps it was Clegg or that new marshal, Barns.

Finally, he stepped out onto the loading platform and looked down into the street. Sidney was standing by the buckboard. Fuller was with her, trying to engage her in conversation.

"Git away from me, Randy Fuller!" Sidney said.

When Fuller saw Potter, he stepped away from Sidney and stared up at him.

"Git away from her, mister," Potter growled down at Fuller.

"I don't think I'll do thet, greener," Fuller said, sarcastically. "Heck, she's my girl!"

Sidney Harnett glared at Fuller. "You lying skunk, Randy Fuller! I wouldn't spit on yer grave!"

Potter stepped slowly and cautiously into the street. He started for the buckboard, but Underwood blocked his path.

"Excuse me, sir," Potter said, "if you'll let me put these staples away, I'll be at yer service."

Underwood turned to his pal Fuller and laughed. "Did you hear thet, Randy? He says he's gonna be at my service. Now ain't thet fancy talk?" Underwood turned back to the young cowboy. "Now you do thet, fancy boy, an' I'll jest step back up the road and we'll see if yer fancy talk is any good."

"Much obliged, mister," Potter said.

He put the sack of groceries in the back of the buckboard and walked a few steps out onto the road. Underwood was walking slowly away. He stopped at about thirty feet, turned and faced Potter, adjusting his gunbelt and flexing his fingers. He took up the stance and smiled confidently.

Sidney looked scared. She rushed to Potter's side and grabbed his left arm. "Let's go, Jake!" Her voice cracked. "Please, let's go home!"

"I'm sorry, I can't, Miss Sidney. He insulted you, an' where I come from a man don't insult a lady."

Fuller had heard. He chuckled. "Where the hell you from, greener?"

Potter gently pushed Sidney aside, putting a good distance between them both. "I'm from Texas," Potter said calmly as he took up the stance. It was his calmness that suddenly began to unnerved Underwood. For a brief moment Tom Underwood looked uncertain. He was now less sure of himself than he had been a moment before. He had braced the young Texan and now he couldn't back down.

So, without warning, he went for his gun, trying to get an edge.

Jake Potter shifted to the right a little and went into a crouch. His gun hand moved with incredible speed, sliding up along his holster and taking the Colt with it. At the same time, his left hand met it at a precise spot and fanned off a single, clean shot.

Even before Underwood could finish his draw, Potter's bullet hit him in the heart, knocking him backwards into a sitting position on the road. He sat there a moment looking surprised and then slowly fell sideways. After that, he didn't move.

Suddenly, there was a second and third shot from behind Potter.

The Texan felt a sting in his shoulder, as if someone had punched him there. He grunted and spun around in time to see Fuller's body slam against the buckboard, bounce off and hit the ground face down. Someone near the mercantile had shot him.

That someone was old Tank Stillwell. He had put a bullet in Fuller, knocking his aim off just as he was about to shoot Potter in the back. The old man walked up to Fuller's body to check it. Satisfied, he walked over to the buckboard.

"He was gonna shoot ya in the back, kid," the old man said. Sidney noticed he wasn't wearing his badge. "You okay?" the old man asked, holstering his gun.

Potter was leaning against the buckboard for support, holding his left arm. It was bleeding up high on his shoulder.

"He's hurt bad!" Sidney whined. She supported the young cowboy to keep him on his feet.

Potter winked at Stillwell and the old man winked back.

"Let's git him over to Doc Stanton's place," Stillwell said, trying to sound urgent.

By now, people had begun to gather in a small crowd all about them. Saul Gains was standing on the ramp in front of the mercantile, looking on.

Sidney and the old man helped Potter across the street to the doctor's place, leaving the townsfolk to gawk at the bodies of Fuller and Underwood. More people came walking down from the Silver Sparrow Saloon. One was Marshal Barns.

"What happened here?" the newly appointed marshal demanded to know.

"These two Circle S men braced a young cowboy," someone said. "Looks like they got the worst of the deal."

"Yeah," another said. "I saw the whole thing. The kid come outta the mercantile with groceries and they braced him fer no reason at all."

A third observer offered, "When the kid beat Underwood, Fuller jumped in. He wounded the kid but old Stillwell put a pill in him."

Barns stood silently fuming, trying to stifle his anger. There wasn't much he could do with all the witnesses swearing it was self-defense. Damn old Stillwell! He'd fix his goose real pronto!

Barns pointed at four Circle S cowboys who stood in the crowd.

"Tie them on their horses, men, an' take 'em back to the Circle S. Tell Spears what happened. I'll be out ta see him later."

Barns thought about going over to the doctor's office and arresting Stillwell and the kid, but decided against it. He'd go see Dan Clegg and get his advice first. He dared not make a move without talking first to the Circle S ramrod. He and Spears were calling the shots.

Barns got on his horse and rode out to the Circle S to see Dan Clegg and tell him what had happened. Clegg would know what to do.

Chapter 12

It was a few hours after the gunfight in town between Potter and the Circle S cowboys. Clegg and Spears were alone in the rancher's den talking. The ramrod had just told his boss what Barns had told him.

"Where's Barns now?"

"I sent him back to town to look for Stillwell and ta kill him," Clegg said. He swore under his breath. "Damnit! Fuller and Underwood were two of our best men."

"Yes, I know," Spears replied. He lit a cigar and blew a billow of gray smoke above Clegg's head. "We'll have to do something about that and right away."

Clegg changed the subject. "Just so ya know, there's talk goin' around about you an' the girl."

Spears' eyes narrowed. He leaned back in his chair, staring hard at Clegg.

"Oh, what kind of talk?" Spears asked. He already figured that rumors about him were going around town, but he didn't know exactly what they were.

"Thet you had me kill Sam Hill because he was messin' around with Gail Simpson behind yer back. Anyway, thet's the story goin' around town now."

Spears' face took on a dark, somber look.

He had felt it, heard the whispers and seen the stares, whenever he went to town. It was especially evident at church with the girl, Gail Simpson, sitting beside him. He was trying to get their acceptance, their approval of her, but they wouldn't give it. He could hear the whispering and snickering when his back was turned. He hated every one of them and he'd show them who ran the town. He'd teach them all a lesson, in the end.

"I don't give a damn about the lot of them." Spears forced a chuckle. "I run this town and they know it. It was dead and I brought it back to life. Without me, there wouldn't be any damn town."

Clegg nodded. He knew it was best not to disagree with Spears. The rancher was totally unforgiving and held a grudge forever. And of late he had been acting strange.

"You're right there, boss," Clegg said, trying to sound sincere. He paused a moment and asked, "Where's the girl?" He hadn't seen her since he'd brought her out to the ranch.

"I keep her upstairs. I bring her down to eat and talk."

Clegg smiled, as if he approved. Actually, he thought Spears was a damn fool for going through all this trouble over the girl. If the truth be told, it was she who had a hold on him, not him on her. He was so besotted and blinded by her, he couldn't even see or think straight. No doubt she hated his guts for having Sam Hill killed.

"She needs time to get over Hill," Spears said, leaning back in his chair, staring at the ceiling as if he thought she could hear him up there in her room. "She'll come around when she realizes she loves me." He paused a moment. "I'm getting her a new fancy necklace from Kansas City. Real diamonds. She'll love it."

In Clegg's mind, that had affirmed what he had been thinking all along. His boss was insanely enslaved by Gail Simpson. To the ramrod this was a sign of weakness, a flaw in Spears' character.

"Sure, that'll do it," Clegg heard himself saying. He knew exactly what the girl was doing, and that was stringing Spears along. He began rolling a cigarette before asking, "But what about Fuller and Underwood?"

"How do the boys feel?"

Clegg finished rolling the cigarette before answering. "They're mad as hell. They want action. So far, I've been able ta hold 'em back."

"Fuller and Underwood were well liked, weren't they?"

"They sure were, boss."

Spears took another deep drag on his cigar and exhaled. His mind was searching for a way to use the death of Fuller and Underwood to get the Diamond H Ranch. Now that Brittney Harnett's husband was gone, it should be easy to take over.

Suddenly his face clouded as he thought about how the man, Logan, had undercut him at the bank.

"I almost had a lien on the Harnett spread," Spears said. "Some meddler named Logan beat me to it. I wonder what his game is?"

"About Logan, boss, one of the cowhands said he recognized him from way back, when he was a card sharp an' a gunslinger."

"Is that so?" Spears asked with interest.

"Yeah, an' someone heard he was connected to a gang called The Gang of Six. They robbed banks."

Spears laughed. "Well, now, isn't that a coincidence? That's great. All you have to do is take some men out there with Marshal Barns and arrest him."

"Ah, it ain't that simple, boss."

"Why not?"

"Trace Logan is supposed to be dead. His gang got caught in an ambush when they robbed the Hays City Cattlemen's Savings and Loan a few months ago."

"I see," Spears said. He reflected on the matter some more. Finally he asked, "But what if the boys decided to get satisfaction for the killing of Fuller and Underwood?"

"Like how?"

"Supposing a posse went out to the Harnett spread. They could legally hang the kid and this Logan fellow. Your man can swear that Logan is a bank robber who rode with the Gang of Six!"

"Would that be legal?"

"Sure. I'm the law here anyway. With Barns as marshal, we can get away with it. We could also arrest both of them Harnett women for harboring a bank robber as well."

"So we take care of the kid, Logan and the women all at once," Clegg said, nodding. "I like that." Then suddenly, "It won't be easy. Some of our boys might get hurt. Some might even git killed."

"Have Barns deputize them. That will make their killing a crime in the eyes of the law. You can hang everyone involved."

"Yeah, I could do thet, couldn't I?"

"I'm doubling your pay, Clegg, to eighty a month." Spears got some money from the den safe and handed it to the ramrod. "See that the boys get plenty to drink before they go out there."

Suddenly Clegg felt a lot better. He took the money and left.

Spears sat alone in his den smoking his cigar. Things were going to get better soon. He could sense it. The Harnett ranch would soon be his. Not that he needed it. It was because he wanted it and he was used to getting what he wanted.

After finishing his cigar, the rancher walked upstairs to where Gail Simpson was locked in her bedroom. He unlocked the door and went in. As soon as she saw him, she jumped off the bed and stood cowering behind a chair with her body trembling. Her arms and legs were bruised where he had beaten her, but not her face. He had not touched that beautiful face.

"Please don't hurt me anymore, Gabe," the girl whined. Spears closed the door behind him. "I'll be a good girl. Don't hurt me anymore, Gabe, please!"

"Only a few more lessons, my love," Spears said as he went towards her.

She began to whimper like a beaten dog.

Chapter 13

After helping Sidney Harnett take Jake Potter over to see the doctor, old Tank Stillwell whispered something to the young Texan and headed for the stables. Sidney and Potter got in the buckboard and rode west for the Diamond H Ranch. It was afternoon when they arrived. They joined Brittney and Logan who were in the kitchen having coffee. The young man's left arm was in a sling. Sidney told Logan and her mother what had happened.

"How bad is it?" Brittney asked.

"Accordin' to Doc Stanton, it ain't thet bad," Potter said. He seemed proud of his wound. "He sewed it up real good."

"Well, you lost a lot of blood," Sidney said. "So you better take it easy fer a few days." She seemed more friendly towards the young cowboy now that he had been wounded defending her honor. It gave her a feeling of being important.

"It was a good thing old Stillwell showed up," Potter said. "Fuller woulda shot me in the back fer sure."

"He was a fine marshal," Sidney said. "The town respected him. Now we have to put up with the one called Barns. Spears and Clegg are behind it all."

"It seems like it, doesn't it?" Brittney said. Then she asked, "Where did Mr. Stillwell disappear to?"

"He told me he was gonna do some snoopin' around," Potter said.

"Snooping?" Brittney asked.

"Yup."

"What kind of snooping?"

"He didn't say," Potter replied.

"He's a bit simple," Sidney offered.

"No, he isn't," Brittney said defensively. "He's pretty darn smart. You don't get to live as long as he has if you're simple."

"I guess," Sidney conceded.

"Mr. Stillwell needs someone to take care of him," Brittney said. "He's all alone."

"Well, I'm sure glad he watched my back in town," Potter chuckled. "I'd be dead now if it wasn't for him."

Logan looked solemn. He spoke up. "I think trouble might be coming yer way, Mrs. Harnett."

Brittney looked surprised. "Why is that, Mr. Logan?"

"What happened in town today will give Spears the excuse he needs to come after you."

"Spears? He wouldn't dare," Sidney said. "At least not out in the open."

"Not out in the open," Logan replied, "but he'll be behind whatever happens next. I'm sure of it. Potter killed two of his men and I've stopped him from getting his hands on your ranch."

The room went quiet for a moment. They listened to the familiar sounds of life, the creaking of the old house, the chickens cackling in the yard and the snorting of the horses in the corral.

"It wasn't Mr. Potter's fault," Sidney finally said. "They came lookin' fer trouble and he gave it to them. He was protecting me, is all."

"And he was right to do that," Logan said. "No, it's not his fault, it's Spears' fault. Him and Clegg. They planned it that way. Now Spears has put his own man in as marshal. He's got the law on his side."

Brittney suddenly stared hard at Logan. The outlaw saw it and waited for her to ask the questions he knew she would eventually ask.

"Yesterday Marshal Barns and his men backed off. They were afraid of you, Mr. Logan. Why was that?"

"Would it matter?"

"Maybe, depending on the reasons," Brittney replied.

Logan saw the serious look on her face. He decided to gamble and tell the truth. "Well, I've got a reputation. I robbed a bank or two a while back."

Brittney was stunned by this outright confession. Her face clouded over.

"There's no reason for stealing other people's money that I can think of," Brittney said sharply. She walked over to the kitchen window and looked out into the yard with her back to Logan.

"Maybe not, but after the bank took our farm in Montana, my mamma died of a broken heart. She'd put all her strength into that little piece of land and so did my daddy. So, we robbed that same bank to give her a decent burial."

"Was it worth it, Mr. Logan?" Brittney said sharply, turning around and glaring at him.

"To us it was. I hope the people who bought the land are God fearing people who'll respect that little grave we left behind."

"And your father? What about him?"

Logan got a distant look in his eyes as he pulled up an image from the past. "Dead. Cozad City, Nebraska. A long time ago. Shot in the back by a posse."

"I'm sorry to hear that, Mr. Logan," Brittney said. She looked at the outlaw with a concerned stare. "And when do you expect to die, sir? Tomorrow? A week from now? When? How long can you hide from the law?"

Sidney blurted out, "Momma! Thet's not right!"

Brittney Harnett's eyes were moist. She choked back her tears. "I'm sorry, Mr. Logan, but I think it best if you move on."

Logan nodded. "Sure, ma'am, I'll leave, if that's what you want." Logan said. His eyes met hers and they locked for a moment.

"Please leave as soon as you can, sir." Her voice cracked. She quickly looked away.

"Mother! Please don't!" Sidney said again, almost pleading.

"Will tomorrow morning be quick enough, ma'am?" Logan asked. "Or should I leave now?"

Brittney Harnett nodded. "Yes. That will be fine." She turned to the young cowboy. "Mr. Potter, seein' as you're wounded, you'd best take a room upstairs where we can keep an eye on you."

Potter glanced at Logan with a conflicted look on his face. The outlaw nodded and the young cowboy turned back to Brittney. "Alright, ma'am, if you want me to."

Logan got up and said, "Evening, ma'am."

He walked slowly out into the yard, stood looking around for a while, then headed for the corral. After getting his horse out he took it into the barn and began brushing it down. "Looks like it's gonna be just you an' me agin, old pal," he whispered. The animal nudged him with its head and whinnied.

Evening was closing in. When he was finished, Logan put his mount back in the corral, went into the bunkhouse and lay on his cot. He had a deep feeling the winds of danger were blowing towards the Diamond H spread. They would come fast and hard and Dan Clegg would be riding out in front.

Chapter 14

After the meeting with Spears, Dan Clegg sent runners to gather in all the hands who weren't out on range duty. He ended up with twelve cowboys, all loyal, especially when fired up with rotgut whiskey. While they were waiting in the bunkhouse by the light of an oil lamp, Marshal Barns came riding up through the evening shadows. He dismounted and walked up to Clegg, who met him in the doorway.

"Howdy, Barns," Clegg said. "I was just about ta get this shindig started."

The marshal nodded and followed Clegg inside. Once there, he sidled over into a dark corner to watch. He knew Clegg was a master at stirring up men.

The room was heavy with cigarette smoke and the smell of whiskey. Clegg already had two of his close pals, Castor and Slopes, standing with the others. He climbed up on a wooden crate and called for attention.

"Alright, men," Clegg yelled. "Settle down an' listen up." He waited until it was quiet, then cleared his throat. "Y'all know why I called ya here."

"Damn right," Castor said loudly on cue. "Fuller and Underwood were gunned down in cold blood by Diamond H boys, thet's why."

"Thet's right," Clegg replied. "They was a-mindin' their own business in town when they were ambushed by a kid named Potter and a sidewinder named Logan. Both are ridin' for the Diamond H brand."

One lone cowboy stood up and said uncertainly, "The way I heard it was, Fuller and Underwood braced the kid in front of Saul Gain's Mercantile and he beat 'em both to the draw."

"Well, that's a lie," Clegg growled. "An outright lie. You heard wrong. Ask Slopes. He saw it all go down, right, Slopes?"

Slopes, a tall, lean, gaunt cowboy with a cigarette dangling from the left side of his mouth stood up. "I sure as heck did!" He squinted narrow-eyed in a threatening way at the other cowboy. "It's jest like Castor says, Fuller and Underwood was bushwhacked. I seen it an' it went down jest like he says."

"Okay, then, I guess it did," the cowboy said sheepishly and sat down.

"Whatta we gonna do about it, boys?" Clegg asked. "Are we gonna jest turn our backs an' forget it, or are we gonna show 'em they can't pull thet stuff on the Circle S? What's it gonna be?"

"We can't let it stand!" Castor yelled.

Barns smiled from the shadows. Clegg knew his stuff. It wouldn't be long before they were all riled up.

"Nobody kin ambush a Circle S cowboy and git away with it!" Slopes growled.

"Hang 'em both!" someone else shouted out.

Clegg held his hand up for quiet again. Finally, he said, "They're sittin' over at the Diamond H spread with them two Harnett harlots laughin' an' dancin' and havin' a good time while Fuller and Underwood grow cold in the grave. Are we gonna jest sit here like yellah bellies an' do nothin'?"

"Hell, no!" The words roared throughout the bunkhouse, bouncing off the walls.

When it died down, Clegg said, "Ta make it legal, Marshal Barns is gonna swear ya all in as lawmen."

Outside, standing by a bunkhouse window unseen, old Tank Stillwell smirked. That was all he needed to hear. He walked from the yard to a nearby field where he had tied his horse, mounted up and rode quickly for the Diamond H Ranch.

Chapter 15

Trace Logan was almost asleep when he heard a horse in the distance. It was coming on fast, but slowed down as it approached the yard fence. It finally stopped on the road and the rider walked the animal the rest of the way in and up to the bunkhouse.

Logan slipped into his clothes and sat on his bunk with his Colt pointed at the door, listening to the approaching footsteps. A few moments later it opened slowly and the bent over silhouette of old Tank Stillwell stood there staring in.

"You ain't gonna drill me, are ya Logan?" Stillwell's rusty voice whispered.

"Come on in, Marshal," Logan said.

The old man ambled in and sat on a bunk across from Logan. "I jest came from the Circle S, Logan. Dan Clegg is stirrin' up a hornet's nest there. An' thet phony Marshal Barns is in on it, too."

"I figured as much," Logan replied, nodding.

"You'd best git set fer a big fight, friend. He'll be comin' with a dozen men, an' most of 'em will be half-drunk an' thet won't be good fer the women, if ya git my drift."

Logan rubbed the sleep from his eyes. "Did you say a dozen?"

"Yep. At least a dozen."

"We can't fight that many. We'll need help."

"I'm the only help yer gonna git, and if they git their greasy hands on the girls, it ain't gonna be pretty, no sir. As fer you an' the kid, yer both gonna hang if they git their way."

"What should we do, Marshal?"

"Git in the house as fast as ya kin and git set up fer a rip-snortin' fight. Thet's all ya kin do."

"Suppose we left the house and went into the woods. Would that work?"

"Ya can't let 'em get close ta tha house. They'd burn it down along with the barn and bunkhouse. No, ya gotta stand an' fight! With me here, we kin lick 'em. I know a trick."

"Yeah? What's that?" Logan asked skeptically.

"I'm gonna fight 'em Injin style," the old man said. "Now, you get ta movin', friend." That was the end of the conversation. The old man got up and disappeared into the night.

Logan got his and Potter's rifles and ran with them up to the house. As the dining room windows gave the widest view of the yard, corral and bunkhouse, he put the rifles in there. He also turned over the big oak dining room table and pushed it up to the windows for a shield. He purposely made a lot of noise, and in a few minutes Brittney, Sidney and Potter came down to stare at him.

Brittney asked, "Have you gone crazy, Mr. Logan?"

"Can you girls shoot?" Logan asked.

"Of course we can," Brittney replied. "Why?"

"Because they're coming for us," Logan said bluntly.

"Who?" Sidney asked. Half awake, she rubbed her eyes.

"Dan Clegg, Marshal Barns and a dozen Circle S men," Logan said. "Tank Stillwell just told me."

"Where is he?" Brittney asked.

"I've no idea, ma'am," Logan replied. "He skittered off somewhere without saying."

Potter finally came awake. He flexed his wounded arm to get the blood circulating.

"How's the shoulder, kid?" Logan asked him.

"It's fine," Potter replied.

"Good. You're gonna be using it real soon."

Potter asked, "Won't we be needin' more guns fer this?"

"We have a few in my husband's den," Brittney said. "Sidney, you blow out all the lights in the house. Mr. Potter, come with me."

"I'll help," Logan said.

Seconds later, Logan, Potter and Brittney were in the den across the hall emptying out a gun case of rifles and shotguns. There were boxes of shells for each weapon. They carried everything into the dining room.

Sidney finally joined them. Brittney handed her a rifle, saying, "This is the one yer Gran'pa gave you. It pulls to the right and up a bit, remember."

"Yes, Momma, I remember," Sidney replied.

Potter cleared his throat. "I guess I created this mess by killin' those Circle S cowboys, didn't I?"

"No," Brittney said. "Spears would have found another excuse, I imagine, so don't fret about it. In fact, this ain't even your fight. You can ride out right now, Mr. Potter. You too, Mr. Logan."

"It's too late to ride out now," Potter said gravely. "Hear that?"

Logan stood at a window listening. The others went to the adjacent window. It sounded like distant thunder rolling in their direction and it steadily got louder.

"That'll be them," Logan said.

Potter grabbed a rifle from the stack on the floor and started loading the magazine. Brittney watched him. "Are you alright, Mr. Potter?" she asked.

"Never been better, ma'am. Thank you fer askin', though."

The pounding of horses stopped in the pine trees in the field across from the yard. There was a three-quarter moon above, which made it easy to see into the distance.

They heard voices. Some were thick with drink.

"They're over in the pines," Logan said softly. "They'll come in behind the bunkhouse, then line up behind the fence."

"You think so?" Potter asked.

As if in answer to his question, they heard the ringing of spurs and the pounding of boots on the ground. Dark figures ran along the fence, twenty yards away. They finally stopped.

"They're in position now," Logan whispered. "Once Clegg has them in place, it'll come. Stay away from the windows until after they fire, then let 'em have it."

Logan had no more than spoken when tongues of flame spouted from the rifles lined up along the fence. The first fusillade was aimed up at the second-floor bedrooms, blowing out the window glass and smashing holes in the side of the house. Clegg thought he was catching everyone asleep in their beds.

"Don't fire yet," Logan said.

The shooting from the fence soon died off. After that, there was a short silence.

"Hey, in the house! You still alive?" Clegg called out.

Before Logan could caution him, Potter shouted back. "You wanna dance with me, Clegg?" Potter yelled. "Meet me in the yard. Jest you an' me!"

They heard Clegg's sarcastic laugh. "What, so Logan can ambush me? Not a chance. I ain't no fool, kid." He paused a moment, then said, "Send the Harnett woman an' her daughter out."

"You can forget that, Clegg. Nobody's coming out," Logan shouted back.

Brittney yelled out from the dining room window, "Clegg, you're on my property. You'd best leave."

"All a you, in the house, listen to me," Marshal Barns yelled, "You're under arrest. Lay down yer weapons an' come out with yer hands up in the air!"

When Potter heard the marshal's voice he chuckled. "It's thet phony marshal thet Spears and Clegg appointed to replace old Stillwell." He paused a moment then yelled out, "If you want us, Barns, come an' get us!"

"Alright then, you had your chance," Barns yelled back.

Rifles roared again. Bullets tore into the wall of the dining room, smashing the glass from the windows and sending it showering into the air. Those inside crouched behind the big oak table. Lead ripped through the outside wall and smacked against the table and stuck there, other rounds zinged past and buried themselves into the far wall.

Logan jumped up and levered off five quick shots at a spot where he had last seen Barns. Someone groaned. Potter followed suit and sent a volley of rounds smashing into the fence. Seconds later the women were firing along with them. They sent a wall of bullets smashing into the attackers.

There was a momentary pause before Clegg and his men returned fire. Those in the house answered them shot for shot. Sometimes the firing from the fence was intense, sometimes sporadic and uneven.

Suddenly one of the attackers lit a torch, leaped over the fence and came running, zig-zagging his way across the yard.

"I got him," Potter said.

He grabbed a double-barreled shotgun, stuck it through the broken window and let loose with both barrels. The buckshot caught the attacker in the chest, lifted him off the ground and sent him flying backwards a full ten feet against the fence where he settled down in a lifeless heap.

"Nice shot, kid," Logan yelled as he took aim at another one coming over the fence. His bullet caught the man in the heart and left him hanging limp over the top rail.

A shout of anger came from Clegg. "Kill them all, men! The women, too!" he screamed.

A torrent of bullets came from the attackers and blasted the house again, shattering what was left of the glass in the windows and cutting pieces of wood out of the big table.

"Down!" Logan yelled. "Kiss the floor!"

They fell flat on the floor, hugging it as hot lead smacked into the table, tearing it to pieces. The fusillade of lead kept coming, tearing the front of the house apart, eating through the wood and into the room.

Suddenly, three gunshots came from a rise looking down on the fence.

"We're bein' ambushed!" someone suddenly shouted. It sounded like Clegg.

There was a shifting of fire away from the house and up at the rise.

"It's Stillwell," Logan yelled. "He's got them in a crossfire!"

Logan got up from the floor and started firing again. The others took up positions at the windows once more and poured lead into Clegg's men, sending a rain of death across the yard into them.

Finally, those inside the house crouched down low to reload and listen. There was no return fire. After a short silence, they heard horses pounding away.

The fight was over.

Logan got up and walked slowly outside, his rifle at the ready. He realized that dawn was breaking in the east. The fight had lasted several hours. He glanced at the bullet-torn fence for a moment and turned to the house.

"Don't come out here!" he shouted.

He counted the bodies of the attackers. Eight lay dead along the fence amid blood stains and empty whiskey bottles. Parts of the fence had been blasted away by bullets.

Old Tank Stillwell came hobbling down from the rise and into the yard. He walked among the bodies until he found what he was looking for. He bent over Barns' limp, bullet-ridden form, removed the marshal's badge from his vest and pinned it on his own, over his heart.

Tank Stillwell looked at Logan and said, "Barns wouldn't make a pimple on a lawman's behind."

Logan nodded in agreement. They walked back into the house and found Sidney kneeling beside her mother. Potter was looking anxiously on.

"She's wounded!" Sidney said, sobbing, trying to lift her mother up.

Logan rushed over and picked Brittney up in his arms and carried her into the kitchen.

"What do you think you are doing, Mr. Logan?" Brittney asked. She smiled weakly, a bit dazed.

"You're wounded in the side."

"I am?" Brittney sounded confused. "I never noticed. Am I dying?"

"No," Logan said.

He sat her on a kitchen chair as Sidney got the medicine box from the sideboard.

"Pull up your mother's shirt, Sid," Logan said.

The bullet had cut a neat, shallow ridge along Brittney Harnett's left midriff. Logan sloshed some alcohol on it. She gasped and inhaled deeply to catch her breath. Then, he wound several layers of gauze bandage around her waist.

"Thank you, Mr. Logan," she said softly, "I feel a lot better now."

"It was my pleasure, ma'am."

"How many dead?" Potter asked.

"I counted eight," Marshal Stillwell replied.

"Jesus!" Potter said.

"Clegg?" Brittney asked. "What about Clegg, Marshal?"

"Let's say the Circle S is gonna need a new ramrod," Tank Stillwell said. "Him an' Barns has both bit the dust. An' I'm takin' my job back." He pointed to the marshal's badge on his vest and chuckled.

"Marshal Stillwell," Sidney said with pride.

The old man nodded. "Heck, them was the dumbest sons-a-guns whatever rode a bronc," Stillwell said. "Shucks, all they had ta do was surround the house, set fire to it and kill you all as ya ran out. Any Injin knows thet."

Potter chuckled. "I'm sure glad they didn't think of it."

As Sidney began making breakfast, Logan rolled a cigarette and thought about how good Brittney Harnett had felt in his arms.

Chapter 16

Gail Simpson stood by her bedroom window staring down at the dark windows of the Circle S bunkhouse on the far side of the yard. It was deserted. Dan Clegg and his men had ridden off about half an hour ago to attack the Diamond H Ranch. She watched, cursing him under her breath, hating him and hoping he would die.

As she stood staring blankly out into the yard, her mind turned to the day Clegg had shot her sweetheart, Sam Hill, in the Silver Sparrow Saloon. She knew that Gabe Spears had ordered him to do the killing. And, when Clegg came to the Bluestem Hotel to get her, she also knew her life was about to become a living hell.

"Pack up, little darlin'," Clegg had chuckled with a sarcastic smirk. Castor and Slopes were with him and they enjoyed knowing she was in for a hell of a beating from Spears. He would show her no mercy.

"Kin I have a little privacy, Dan?" she had asked Clegg, fluttering her eyelashes like a cute little girl.

"Sure, darlin'," Clegg had said. "Take yer time."

They had gone out into the hall to have a smoke and snicker as they waited, joking about what Gabe Spears would do to her. Gail slowly packed her belongings, most of which Spears had bought her, although she did have some small things given to her by her lover, Sam Hill. In half an hour, she was packed.

The last thing she did before leaving was to look in the mirror and adjust her fancy bonnet to make sure it was on right. Once she was satisfied, she picked up the long, steel, silver plated hat pin with its teardrop shaped pearl-handle and thrust it through the bonnet to hold it in place. Her beautiful blonde hair was tucked neatly up into it, revealing her slender, white neck.

Spears bought the elegant bonnet for her right after they met in Kansas City. That was when he swept her off her feet and he was the biggest thing in her dull, common life.

In the beginning, Spears had excited her. He courted her with gifts of candies and pulp magazines about love, romance and adventure. As time went on, she saw what a narrow-minded man he was. Solemn and brooding, he often raved for hours about his schemes of grandeur, his plans to become a leader of men. Eventually she felt like she was nothing but an outlet for his primal pleasures, a concubine he kept hidden in a smelly hotel room, to be used once a week for his private pleasure.

After a while she began to feel a hollowness, an emptiness in her life. Being the mistress of a rich man was fine, but it didn't fill her own emotional needs. Needs that Spears could never satisfy.

Then, one day, an exciting young cowboy named Sam Hill came along and made her feel alive. Even the danger of meeting him in secret didn't stop her. He was a good natured, happy-go-lucky cowboy full of fun and laughter, the opposite of stuffy, boring Gabe Spears.

Gail planned to tell Spears that she was in love with the young, vibrant cowboy, that it was all over between them and he should pay more attention to his wife. But she never got the chance. Spears' wife died, Dan Clegg killed Sam Hill and now here she was, a prisoner at the Circle S Ranch.

Spears allowed her very little freedom of movement at the Circle S. He always had either Clegg or one of Clegg's close friends keep an eye on her whenever she left the house to get some fresh air.

Every evening she and Spears would sit at the long dining room table with Clegg and a couple of his selected cowboys. They would be served by Jeffries, the violin playing cook whom Spears had enticed away from a restaurant in Hays City with an offer of more money and less work. Candles were lined up on the table and everyone was forced to drink the wine Spears had shipped in from

California. None of them liked it. Their preference was either rotgut or hard cider.

Looking very elegant and handsome in his dark suit, white shirt and black tie, Jeffries would serve the special meal he had prepared, then stand in a corner out of sight and wait. When everyone was finished, he would quietly clear the table. He seldom talked to anyone. The cowboys didn't like him very much and treated him as if he were their inferior.

Jeffries also had another duty and that was, after the meal was over and the cowboys had left, he would play slow, romantic waltzes on his violin so that Gail and Spears could dance. Playing a violin was one of Jeffries' many talents that Gail liked and enjoyed.

When the dancing was over, Spears would take Gail Simpson upstairs to her bedroom and Jeffries would go to his small nook behind the larder. Sometimes he could hear her sobbing upstairs in her room, after Spears had beaten her. When Spears was away, he offered her what comfort he could. They quickly became close friends.

On the night Dan Clegg took his men out to raid the Harnett ranch, Spears canceled the formal dinner. With everyone gone and darkness setting in, an eerie quiet fell over the ranch house. The rancher had Jeffries cook him and Gail a light supper, but there was no music or dancing. When the meal was over, the rancher locked Gail up in her room and went back down to his study to do some paperwork. Jeffries went to his room and took to reading a book of poems.

As for Spears, he was giddy with expectation. In a few hours Clegg and the Circle S cowboys would come riding back to report that his mission was accomplished.

The story to be circulated by Marshal Barns was that the Harnett women, Brittney and her daughter Sidney, were in cahoots with bank robber Trace Logan and his sidekick, Jake Potter, two notorious criminals. When the marshal went out to arrest them, they barricaded themselves in the ranch house and fired on the posse. In the ensuing fight, everyone in the house was killed. It was a neat, clean and simple story everyone would believe.

Bored with the paperwork, Spears smoked a cigar and sipped a glass of bourbon. When he was finished, he stretched, blew out the lamp and went out into the darkened hall. He stood looking up at the second-floor landing for a moment, smiled and then walked slowly up the stairs and down the hallway to Gail's bedroom. Unlocking the door, the rancher looked in to see her sitting in a chair reading a magazine by lamplight.

The light fell on her golden hair and she looked especially lovely in her pink chemise. His senses caught the aroma of that expensive perfume he had ordered for her from New York. He was feeling giddy and euphoric.

As he closed the door behind him and approached her, she dropped the magazine and backed away like a cornered animal.

"No, no, my dear," Spears said. "Don't be afraid. This is a special night, my love. There will be no lessons."

Gail saw the strange, odd look on his face. That condescending smile she hated so much was gone. It had been replaced by something different, a delusional look she had never seen before. It was a look that frightened her.

"No," Spears went on saying, "tonight will be a different night, my darling. A night of passion and love. Doesn't that excite you, my love?"

"Yeah, sure, Gabe," Gail blurted out, more terrified than ever. It was as if someone else had taken possession of Spears' body and mind. His eyes seemed to pull back deeper into their sockets and send out a fanatical fire.

He kept walking slowly in a circle around the room, talking about owning the entire valley, of crushing all the small ranchers and taking all their lands for himself.

This sudden change in Spears terrified Gail. She looked frantically around the room for a place to hide or escape, even though she knew there was none. She was at her wits end, submitting to him again now seemed agonizingly unbearable. He had destroyed every vestige of affection she'd ever had for him.

Then her eyes suddenly rested on the bonnet that lay on the top of the dresser. A calmness fell over her. She suddenly saw a way out of this hell she had been cast into. The shell of fear dissolved and fell from her. She knew now what she must do to get free.

Slowly making her way to the dresser, Gail turned her back to Spears and carefully ran her fingers over the outside contours of the bonnet. They roamed across its surface until they found the long, steel, pearl-handled hat pin used to keep the wind from blowing the bonnet off her head.

She was ready when Spears came up behind her, pressing hard against her with his hands around her waist.

"Soon, I'll own everything in this valley, just as I own you," he said as he spun her around roughly and crushed his mouth against hers.

She fell limp in his arms, offering no resistance or help, staring past his face, not wanting to see that strange look on it. He was very rough as he began to take her. She gasped in pain and stiffened.

"No!"

Her right hand came up with the hat pin, searching for its target.

For a moment, he thought a wasp had stung him in his left ear, but quickly realized what she had done. He let out a roar and reached up to choke her, but his fingers had no strength in them. It was too late, the damage had already been done. His eyes could no longer focus and his body began to feel strangely cold and heavy.

Gail let out an agonized sob. Trembling, she held his arm and helped him over to a chair. He very cautiously sat down with a confused look on his face. She stared into his eyes, watching the fire in them slowly fading. Just before the glow of life disappeared, Spears let out a long, heavy sigh. Blood began to trickle from his ear and nose, drip-dropping onto his expensive evening jacket. The girl held his hand as his body settled back in the chair and fell limp. She cried for a long time before she wiped the hat pin clean on Spears' clothes and put it back in the bonnet.

"Gabe," she sobbed. "I'm so sorry it turned out like this, honey. I have ta go now, so goodbye, darlin'."

Later that night, under cover of darkness, she and Jeffries removed all the money from the safe in Spears' den. When they were sure the bunkhouse was dark and quiet, they silently saddled up two horses and a pack animal with food, supplies and his violin and rode north for Nebraska.

Gail Simpson planned to put Kansas behind her and waltz her way back to Montana, where she was born.

Chapter 17

It was the morning after the shootout at the Harnett spread. Breakfast was over and Logan and the marshal had gathered up all the loose horses and tied the bodies of the dead across their saddles. Potter had gone back in the house to rest. The marshal was busy tying the reins of the horses to make a caravan as Logan stood on the porch with his hat in his hand talking to Brittney.

"I want you to know that I respect what you said about bank robbers, ma'am."

"I'm glad you do, Mr. Logan," Brittney said. She stared into his eyes "I could never love such a man."

He was trying to say goodbye, but somehow couldn't find the right words. "I have the utmost respect for you, ma'am," Logan repeated. Then to make her smile, he added, "But please don't go around shootin' men in bars again."

That remark brought a smile to her lips. She looked up into his face, thinking she would never see him again, all because she had put a barrier between them with her harsh condemnation. Neither one knew how to come out and say what they felt deep down inside, what they really wanted to say. They left those words unsaid, knowing they would regret doing so.

Logan put his hat on and walked down into the yard to join the marshal. They mounted up and rode out, pulling the Circle S horses behind. They'd drop the bodies off in town.

Potter and Sidney came out on the porch.

"Take good care of them, kid!" Logan yelled back.

"Ain't ya comin' back?" Potter yelled across the now empty yard. He looked as if he was losing his best friend.

Brittney Harnett shaded her eyes as she stared after the small caravan growing smaller in the distance.

"I'm afraid he's not coming back, Mr. Potter," she said.

The young cowboy nodded. "Yeah, I kinda got the feelin' we ain't gonna see him agin, ever."

Sidney began to cry. She ran into the house. Brittney stared at the young Texan. "And you, Mr. Potter? What about you?" she asked.

Potter looked back at her. "I'd like ta stay on, if ya don't mind."

"I can't offer you any pay."

"It ain't fer the money."

"Is it because of Sidney?" Brittney asked. Potter shrugged. "How does she feel?"

Potter suddenly perked up. "Well, I ain't one fer braggin', but I think my chances are pretty fair in that area, ma'am."

Brittney smiled. She had been watching the two of them and knew the young Texan's prospects were very good with her daughter.

"There'll be little time for romancing, Mr. Potter," she said, trying to sound business like. "There's lots of work to be done around here. And maybe there's a Diamond H bull or heifer still out there roaming around, waiting to be found. If so, then we'll have to find them. They're our only hope."

Potter already knew about the past freeze and the rustlers. If a bull and some cows were to be found, they could be the start of a new herd. But the chances of that were not good. It wasn't very likely to happen. It was hoping against hope.

Brittney stared again at the young cowboy. "Are you really a Texan or are you just saying it?"

"No, ma'am. I wouldn't lie about something like thet," Potter replied with pride.

Brittney nodded and Potter saw the approval in her eyes. "I'll go check on Sidney," she said and went into the house.

Potter stood alone on the porch staring across the empty yard where, a few moments ago, he watched his best friend ride out of his life forever.

Chapter 18

It only took a day to discover rancher Gabe Spears was dead and that Gail Simpson and Jeffries the cook had disappeared. A Circle S cowboy was sent into town to get the marshal but since the marshal was gone, he came back with Doc Stanton. It didn't take the old prairie doctor long to discover that Spears had been murdered. The method used and the fact that Gail Simpson was missing told Doc Stanton who the murderer was. He had known the girl and liked her. He also knew that Spears was mistreating her and that went against the code.

Doc Stanton decided to keep the lid on things. Spears should have been hanged a long time ago anyway. The universe had decided to hold the rancher to account and it was best to leave it at that. So, the good doctor told the Circle S cowboys that Spears died of a heart attack and rode off in his buckboard smiling. He knew why Gail Simpson had taken her revenge and his sympathies lay with her.

After Doc Stanton left, the Circle S cowhands quickly went to work burying Spears' body out back of the big white ranch house. After that they sent word out to the cowhands in the field that the rancher was dead and they should come in. By evening of that same day, fifteen cowboys were assembled in the Circle S bunkhouse. Slick Brewer, a crusty old warhorse, took charge. He was one of the oldest and most respected cowpunchers on the spread. He had been with the Circle S since its earliest days.

"Boys," Brewer lamented, "it's all over fer us. Spears is dead an' so are Dan Clegg and his men. We're all thet's left." Brewer stopped to chuckle. "Looks like Spears hit thet little girl once too often an' the lord struck him down."

"He had it comin'," someone said. "She didn't deserve bein' treated like a dog."

Someone else said. "Well, it looks like he got his cinch tightened up good an' proper." Chuckles followed that observation.

"So, what's gonna happen to the spread, Slick?"

"It'll go to whoever has a claim on it, a relative maybe."

"He ain't got no relatives," another replied. "Clegg said so onct."

"Then it's up to the law an' the court," Slick answered.

"I heard in some cases the county comes in and takes over and sells it off. They takes a cut."

A flop-eared cowboy stood up and asked the question that was in everybody's mind. "What the heck happened ta Clegg an' his boys?"

Slick pulled a plug of tobacco from his shirt pocket and bit off a chew. After getting it under control, he chuckled. "Well, it looks like they rode right into a sledgehammer. Damn if they didn't git taught a lesson. Eight outta twelve bit the dust, as I heard it. An' the other four are still runnin' fer cover."

"Where'd thet happen?" another asked.

"Out at the Diamond H. Somehow, Clegg got the idea of goin' out there an' gettin' revenge fer the killin' of Fuller an' Underwood."

"Well, it sure didn't work out so good fer them, did it, Slick?" someone replied.

Brewer tucked the tobacco cud in one jaw and spit juice into a tin can. He wiped his chin and smiled. "An now it looks like ol' Tank's got his badge back. Good fer him. We was pards, onct."

"Clegg wouldn't a-gone out ta the Diamond H on his own," another said. "Spears must of put the bee in his bonnet. No, sir, he wouldn't a-acted on his own."

"Maybe we should do somethin'," someone else said. "After all, them was our boys what got shot."

120

Slick saw what direction that conversation might be leading so decide to nip it in the bud.

"Listen," Brewer said, "Clegg and his pals had it easy while we busted our rear ends out with the herds night an' day, seven days a week. We broke our backs fer twenty a month while Clegg and his pals rode the gravy train. We don't owe him or Fuller or Underwood a thing. Nor Castor or Slopes, neither. An' surely not Spears."

There was a moment of sober silence, then nods and words of agreement. No further discussion on that subject was required.

"What about the herd?" someone asked. That was the big question.

Brewer replied, "As far as the Circle S herd goes, it's branded an' we can't touch it. But I know of another herd of about thirty thousand head or more, an' it ain't branded. They is cows an' bulls from all the other spreads in the area. Clegg an' his boys were cullin' unbranded cows from them fer years. They even stole unbranded Circle S cows as well. Him an' his boys would sell them on the cheap up in Stockton an' Colby. I suspect Spears never knew what Clegg was up to, bein' as he never rode the range in the last few years."

The old cowpoke paused for a moment to clear his throat, then went on.

"Clegg and his boys was pullin' a fast one on all of us fer a long, long time. They hid thet herd up in the north sector in a small valley where a branch of the Smoky ran. It's about doubled in size by now, seein' as it has about five hundred bulls. I reckon there's maybe thirty thousand head in there now."

"Heck, if ya ask me, I think we got somethin' comin ta us," someone said. "Anyway, nobody's gonna miss a herd that nobody even knows about."

"Hell, let's jest take it fer ourselves and leave this place, instead of sittin' around scratchin' our behinds."

Slick thought about that as he spit his cud into the tobacco can. Finally, he shrugged. "Yeah, I guess we are gettin' the lousy end of the stick."

"We deserve better, Slick," someone else said.

Another cowboy suggested, "Why not jest round 'em up and head 'em south fer Mexico? They buy unbranded mavericks an' don't even ask fer paperwork. Heck, I heard they don't ask any questions, an' they pay five dollars a head, too."

After a long discussion, it was concluded they would take the herd to Mexico. They felt they had something coming for all their years of low wages and hard work.

The next morning Slick Brewer got the gears quickly rolling and soon the Circle S cowpokes were preparing for their final trail drive. They planned to take as much as they could, including the remuda and the chuck wagon. They took the entire larder from the house and all the extra riding gear and trail equipment from the barn. By nightfall, they were packed and ready to leave for Mexico.

In the morning, as they left the ranch house yard, someone suggested, "Let's burn the ranch house down."

"No," Brewer said. "It'll only attract attention. As it is, they'll figure we jest up an' left ta look fer work someplace else. We don't want the law ridin' down our backs."

Old Brewer led his men out across Circle S land, land that had been their whole universe for years. They knew every water hole, every hollow and every bog from one end to the other. They knew where the cows bunched up in winter and gathered to drink in the summer. They knew where every rock lay and where every prairie dog hole was. They had dedicated their lives to riding for the brand even though they got very little in return except the companionship of their fellow cowboys.

They rounded up the phantom herd and moved it out, sixty thousand head. Three days later they were about forty five miles south of the Circle S Ranch.

Chapter 19

Marshal Stillwell and Trace Logan walked into the office of County Sheriff Martin Farrell in Hays City. Logan had a saddlebag slung over his shoulder. The sheriff was talking to a deputy when he glanced over at the doorway and saw them. For a moment he was uncertain who it was.

Stillwell smiled and saluted his friend. "Hi, Marty!" he said.

"Well, I'll be darned!" the sheriff shouted. "Phil, go check on the town while I talk to my pard from the good old days."

As the deputy ran off, the sheriff came forward and shook hands with old Stillwell. They patted each other on the back, ignoring Logan.

"Where the heck you been, ya old skinflint? I ain't seen you since we rode with the Regulators. We sure kicked butts, didn't we?" Farrell and Stillwell were about the same age.

"We sure did, Marty, we sure did!" Stillwell said. "Them was the good ol' days!"

"Where you been, pard?"

"I gave it all up fer wranglin', Marty. I couldn't take all thet killin' no more."

"Yeah, I get yer meanin', pard. I finally did the same, too." The sheriff looked at Logan. "Who's yer friend?" Farrell gave Logan the once over, sizing him up. The outlaw removed his hat so the sheriff could get a good look at him.

"This is Trace Logan." Stillwell said and waited for the sheriff's reaction. "Maybe ya heard a him."

"Can't say as I have. Why?"

"He was the leader of the Gang of Six."

"The hell you say! They robbed the Cattlemen's Savings and Loan here a while back. We killed them all, but never got the money back. Seems like one of them escaped."

"Well, this is him. The leader, Trace Logan."

"How come you ain't got the sidewinder in chains, Tank?" He drew his gun and pointed it at Logan.

"Take it easy, Marty. Logan is givin' himself up an' is askin fer amnesty 'er clemency 'er whatever ya kin offer him," Stillwell said.

"I don't know about that," the sheriff replied, putting his gun back in its holster. "There has to be a reason."

Stillwell pulled some papers from his shirt pocket and handed them to the sheriff.

"What's this?"

"Statements from me and owners of the Diamond H Ranch tellin' how Logan saved their lives. I was there, right in the middle of it."

The sheriff stared at Logan. The outlaw knew a plan was forming.

"Sit down and let's talk," the sheriff said.

Logan laid the saddlebag on the sheriff's desk. He and Stillwell pulled chairs up and sat down.

"It's all there," Logan said, "the thirty-five thousand. Count it."

The sheriff stared at the saddlebag for a moment, then opened it and poured out the money. It took a while to make the count. Finally, he nodded, satisfied.

"Is there a reward for the money's return?" Stillwell asked.

"A thousand dollars," Farrell replied.

"I'll take it and split it with you, seein' as we're pards."

The sheriff thought about that for a moment. "Sure, seeing as we're pards."

"We'll need a pardon kit, then." Stillwell said.

"Sure."

"I mean the whole thing, seal, stamp an' all. The whole works."

"The whole works," the sheriff replied. "Stamp, seal and all. Fingerprints, too. I'll make your boy as clean an' legal as a sky pilot."

"Then let's do 'er," Stillwell chuckled.

It took an hour to fill in the preprinted forms, including the fingerprints. Once it was stamped with the seal of the governor's office, it was done.

"How many of these you do a year?" Logan asked,

"Quite a few. It's really good to get all you sidewinders back on the side of the law. Did you read that last paragraph, Logan?"

"No? Should I?"

"It doesn't matter, now, but it says you'll be hung by the neck until dead if you rob another bank. No jail time. Just a hanging."

"Why the three copies?" Logan asked.

"You get one, I get one and one goes to the state capital. It's all the Governor's program to get you fellahs straight. Once I rode the outlaw trail, too, Logan. So, did Tank, but we came in to work for the law an' we're glad we did, right, Tank?" Stillwell nodded.

"You were an outlaw?" Logan asked the sheriff.

"I robbed trains. I had a good reason, but that's all in the past now."

"I had a good reason for robbing banks, too," Logan said. "Now it's all in the past, too."

The sheriff shook Logan's hand.

Logan waited at the jailhouse while Stillwell and the sheriff went up to the bank to return the money. An hour later they came back and split the reward between them. Stillwell handed his five hundred to Logan.

"How come?" Logan asked

"You'll have a better use fer it than I will."

Once outside and riding west again, the old marshal smiled at Logan. "How's it feel ta be legal?"

"Great. Really great."

Stillwell tossed a metal object at Logan. He caught it and saw it was a deputy's badge.

"How come?"

"Jest in case," Stillwell answered. "It might come in handy."

Logan chuckled and pinned it on his shirt, inside his coat, out of sight. "Sure," he said, "just in case."

They were about twenty miles west of Hays City, heading back to the Diamond H Ranch, when they ran into the Circle S cowboys and the herd.

Chapter 20

The old lawman saw tracks and pointed down at them. At first Logan wasn't sure what he was pointing at or why. "How many?" Logan asked.

"I figure fifteen, maybe even twenty thousand. Could be more. Maybe a dozen men ridin' herd. They got the whole works, includin' a grub wagon."

"How come they're headed south?" Logan asked. "Most trail drives head north to Ellsworth or Dodge."

"They're headed fer Mexico ta sell stolen stock. A good look at the brand might help with thet question." Stillwell looked off into the distance. "Let's go take a look."

They headed southwest. In an hour, they began to feel the earth shake. Later they caught the smell of the herd as its scent drifted back to them on the air currents. Later they came up a small rise and saw the herd bunched up below in a wide gully. There were about nine outriders keeping the cows in tight for the coming of darkness.

"What's the next move?" Logan asked.

"We'll wait until they make camp fer the night," the marshal said. "We'll see who it is."

Logan nodded. "Sure."

Riding slowly along to the left of the herd, Logan and the old man found a place to rest and wait. Around dark they saw the lights of the chuck area and moved in closer. They could smell the bacon and biscuits. They dismounted thirty feet out from the camp.

"I know these men," Marshal Stillwell said, speaking in a soft voice. "They're Circle S cowboys."

"Did you notice these cows aren't branded, Marshal?" Logan whispered.

The marshal nodded "Yeah. They're the ones Clegg and his boys was cullin' from all the ranches fer tha past six years."

They decided to walk into camp and find out what was going on.

"Marshal Stillwell, comin' inta camp!" the marshal said loudly.

Without waiting for an answer, the marshal walked boldly into camp with Logan following. Caught off guard, the Circle S boys sat on the ground slack-jawed and at a loss as to what to do next.

The marshal recognized Slick Brewer. "Howdy, Slick," the marshal said. "This Clegg's herd?"

"It was, Tank, but since he an' and his boys is pushin up daisies, I reckon they won't miss 'em."

"So you an' some of the boys decided ta leave Spears high and dry, huh?"

"I guess you ain't heard, Tank. Spears is dead."

Stillwell's interest perked up. "Dead, ya say? How come?"

"Accordin' to the Doc, his rotten heart jest' plumb gave up the ghost."

The old lawman chuckled. "Heck, then I don't have ta arrest the skunk, do I?"

Slick Brewer stood up. "You ain't gonna try ta arrest us, are ya, Tank? We go way back, if ya remember."

"I remember, Slick. We rode the range fer years on the back sector. We got pissy-faced drunk tagether and we had good an' bad times. Maybe we kin make a deal both of us kin swaller."

"Whatta ya have in mind, Tank?"

"We'll take ten thousand cows and a hundred bulls. You go ahead an' take the rest."

"An if we don't?"

132

"Then you'll have ta talk to my deputy about thet. His name is Trace Logan. He used ta be an outlaw."

"Yeah, I heard of him," Slick replied. "An' I don't want no part of him, Tank. There's about thirty thousand beeves in there. You kin take fifteen thousand and some bulls."

"Thet's mighty darn Christian of ya, Slick," Stillwell replied and they shook hands.

Logan stepped up to the fire and said, "The Diamond H is hiring. Right now it needs four men. Thirty a month, with bunk and bread. Anybody interested?"

Slick Brewer looked at his men. "It's okay. You thet have girlfriends back in Slocum's Ridge might wanna seriously consider the offer. At least sleep on it."

Four men instantly came forward and shook hands with Logan.

"Now that thet's done an' settled," Slick said, "welcome ta camp, Tank. You an' yer pal get a plate an' let's all eat."

The crisis was over and everyone was happy about the outcome. They ate, talked and drank around the campfire. A cowboy played soft music on the harmonica. The night crew went out on herd duty and things settled down. Eventually the fire went out and they all slept for a few hours only to get up at sunrise.

It took two days to cut out the cows and form them into a separate herd. The following day, before the marshal, Logan and the four new men left, Slick Brewer and Tank Stillwell talked.

"Ya won't tell Mrs. Harnett about us, will ya, Tank?"

"No, but I got a notion she knows what went on. It was all Clegg's doin'."

"Thanks. I wouldn't want her ta be thinkin' nothin' bad about me," Brewer said.

"I'll leave it lay. No reason ta tell her."

"I'd be grateful, Tank. I liked her a lot."

For a moment, they stared at one another. There was nothing more to talk about.

"Well, Slick, this is adios," Stillwell said. "You'd best git ta Mexico as fast as ya kin. If ya git caught in Texas with them cattle an' no papers, you'll most likely hang. The whole lot of ya. So, adios and good luck, Slick."

They shook hands. Stillwell rode back to where the four cowboys and Logan were waiting with the cattle. They headed northwest for Slocum's Ridge.

They moved the herd fifteen miles a day without any mishaps. When they were five miles out from the Diamond H, they stopped.

"I'll ride in an' tell them what's a-comin' their way," the marshal said. "I don't want 'em all ta drop dead when we come pushing fifteen thousand head of cattle their way."

"Sounds like a good idea," Logan said.

"These four men, they pretty well know the lay of the land on the Diamond H. They've stole enough cattle there, so they know what ta do."

"Alright," Logan said. "I'll follow them in and across to the graze."

Tank Stillwell nodded and rode ahead. Logan rode back and told the lead man, Ed Carey, to push the herd on to the middle graze of the Harnett spread. It was still a two-hour job and the men got back to the Diamond H yard just before sundown. The marshal had already left for town so Brittney took Logan off to the side to talk.

"The marshal said you brought back fifteen thousand head, Logan. Is it true?"

"Yes, ma'am, it is," Logan replied. "For about six years Clegg and his men had been culling off a few hundred at a time to build up a secret herd of their own. They're parked out on your range, right now. From what I saw, they're in pretty good shape. There are also a hundred seed bulls in the count."

"Those new cowhands, I can't afford to take them on. You know my situation."

"I'm leaving Potter five hundred dollars. That'll keep them on for six months."

Brittney looked away, avoiding Logan's eyes. "This is the third time you've helped me, Mr. Logan. I wish there was a way I could properly thank you."

Logan looked at her and chuckled. "I could think of a way, ma'am, but I best not say it."

Brittney Harnett caught his meaning and stared into his eyes. "Don't be bashful, Mr. Logan."

Logan was caught flat footed by the quick reply. He wasn't sure how to respond just then so he remained silent. He wanted to take her hand and tell her everything would be alright, but he held back.

Brittney invited the four new cowboys and Logan into the ranch house for smoked ham, sweet potatoes, pole beans and gravy. For dessert, they had rhubarb tarts and coffee. After that she talked to the cowboys and introduced Potter as their ramrod. He took them down to the bunkhouse. They stowed their gear and then took care of their horses. After leaving their mounts in the corral they went back to the bunkhouse to play cards and talk about their sweethearts in town.

Because she helped Sidney with cleaning up the kitchen, Brittney didn't get a chance to talk to Logan again. When they were finished, she looked around but couldn't find him. A sudden feeling of panic came over her and she knew her heart was telling her something she already knew, but had denied. Maybe he had ridden off. After the way she had treated him, she couldn't blame him. Her blunt honesty had hurt him and she now regretted every word. She had seen the pain in his eyes that day. He could have rebuked her, but he didn't. Instead, he took it and kept silent, not wanting to anger her.

Suddenly she rushed out onto the porch and looked around the yard. She could hear Potter talking to the new men in the bunkhouse. They were joking and laughing. Thinking Logan might be there with him, she hurried down the porch steps and across the yard. She stopped at the open door of the bunkhouse, undecided as to what she should do. Potter noticed her and came out.

"Can I help you, ma'am?" he asked. He saw the anxious look on her face and instantly guessed what caused it.

Brittney didn't know how to respond. What could she say, that she was hunting for Logan? She smiled and walked away saying, "Never mind, Mr. Potter."

"If yer lookin' fer Trace Logan, he's down in the barn, ma'am," Potter said, smiling.

"I never said I was looking for Mr. Logan, did I, Mr. Potter?" she replied, trying to sound indifferent.

"No, ma'am, you truly didn't. But I figured maybe you'd be wantin' ta say goodbye to him before he rode off."

Brittney gave a start, turned and hurried away towards the barn. With her back still to the young Texan, she said, "Thank you."

She continued walking down to the barn and found Logan inside brushing his horse. She came up close behind him and said, "Tank Stillwell told me about your pardon."

"It was all his doin', ma'am."

"I can't tell you how much it means to me, your cleaning up your past like that, Mr. Logan."

"Does it?"

"Yes, it does."

"Then we're square, ma'am?"

"More than square, Mr. Logan."

Logan stopped brushing the animal and turned slowly to face Brittney. "Good, I wouldn't want to ride off with you thinkin' bad things about me."

"You're leavin'?" she asked. Her heart started jumping again.

"I reckon, unless you've got use for a reformed bank robber."

"Maybe I do," she said. Then, "Yes, I do have use for a reformed bank robber."

She came close to him and put her hand on the horse's neck, near his. They stared at each other. Suddenly, the horse shifted sideways, forcing Logan up against her. She held her ground and he kissed her. She backed off a moment to decide what to do, then came in to be kissed a second time.

"Please don't go, Logan," she whispered.

"Are you sure?"

"Yes, very sure."

Logan bent and kissed her again. "Call me Trace," he said.

"Call me Britt," she whispered in his ear.

Brittney heard Sidney calling for her from the porch. She decided not to answer.

They heard the cowboys talking and laughing up in the bunk house. It was very quiet and peaceful in the barn.

The End

Other western books by R. Annan

Fight for the Lazy M
The Red Bandana
The Cowboy from Sierra Blanca
The Salvation of Trace Logan

Jack Cordell Westerns

The Gunfighter in Winter
Long Ride to Hell's Kitchen
Owl Hawks
Gunfight at Barfield Springs
Shootout at Sanctuary City
Last Days of a Gunfighter

Clay Jared Westerns

Copperhead Moon
Cowboys of the Box R
Prisoners of Brimstone Pass
Range War in C Minor
Devil Wind
Showdown at Wamego Falls
Lightning Riders
Winter Kill
Gunfight at Wild River
Shootout at Rattlesnake Flats

About the Author

R. Annan is a well-traveled author with many interests. As a career serviceman, he served in Korea and Vietnam. He also completed a one-year course at the Defense Language Institute in Monterey, California, and graduated from the University of South Florida with a B.A. in Art and Art History. After taking a two-year course in screenwriting at the Hollywood Scriptwriting Institute, he established The Old Time Radio Club Time Machine as both a scriptwriter and an actor.

As a young boy growing up in the city, R. Annan never passed up a chance to see a western movie. His heroes were Buck Jones, Johnny Mack Brown, Wild Bill Elliot and John Wayne, to name a few. As an adult, he often wondered where his love of westerns came from. Perhaps it has something to do with his grandfather, John L. Annan, who was a cowboy from Helena, Montana, in days of old.

A Note from the Author

Thank you for reading my book. Would you please consider rating and reviewing it? I'd enjoy your feedback. Thank you!